For

L

Lynn Armstrong - Hobbs

xxx

CW00926853

First published in Great Britain in 2011 by Lynne Armstrong-Hobbs

Copyright © Lynne Armstrong-Hobbs 2011

The publisher has asserted her moral rights to be identified as the author.

A CIP Catalogue of this book is available from the British Library

ISBN: 978-0-9565211-4-9

Illustrated by Sue Navin

Cover designed and typeset in Fairfield 11½pt
by Chandler Book Design
www.chandlerbookdesign.co.uk

Printed in Great Britain by the
MPG Books Group, Bodmin and King's Lynn

For Holly and Victoria
who make every day magical

Contents

One Magic Dragon
One Hundred Tiny Horses
and
One Thousand Evil Thworgs

Chapter One

The Chinese Green Dragon

Stormy rain had poured down for days, making it too wet and muddy to play outside, even though it was June and the beginning of summer.

'I hope this rain stops for the weekend!' Holly said to her sister, as they cleared away their breakfast plates. Both girls desperately wanted to talk to the animals in the magic garden and see their friends, the tiny stick people, and especially Mr Leafblower who always made them laugh.

Holly smiled as she remembered how they had first met Mr Leafblower, who lived in a tunnel under the compost heap, and the fun they had had riding on his leaf flume.

Jolting her out of her thoughts, she heard her Mum and Dad talking, and what she heard set her heart racing.

'It sounded like voices calling out - honestly!' Mum sounded amused; and then Holly heard her father laugh loudly and say,

'Well I'm fairly sure we don't have people camping out on our roof! It will be birds, or maybe even squirrels I'll bet.'

Her mum laughed again, and they moved into the dining room and started to discuss Aunty Susan's visit next week.

Holly ran upstairs so fast she nearly fell back down again and had to grab the banister to steady herself. Then, hurling herself through Victoria's bedroom door and onto her bed, she explained breathlessly what she had heard their parents saying.

Vikki knew at once what this might mean: that the animals of the garden were trying to contact them!

All of the animals in the garden could talk to the children but, of course, only when they were all in the garden together; maybe they were using the chimney to try to get in touch. After all, once fully indoors, the animals lost the ability to talk like humans. Staying outside and shouting down the chimney could have been one way of communicating with the children in 'human speak.'

What could be so important that their animal friends

would be trying so hard to talk to them? And why hadn't Monty, their pet cat and the guardian of the animals who lived in the magic garden, tried to alert them?

It was then that they both realised they hadn't actually seen Monty in the house much lately. Together, they headed downstairs.

Holly knelt down by the empty fire grate in the sitting room and leaned her head in as far as she could, hoping to see something up the chimney. But as she looked up all she could see were the dusty grey bricks lining the inside of the chimney - nothing else at all, and certainly no animals.

But after a while of straining her ears, Holly thought she **could** hear a voice from above. Yes, she was now quite sure - without any doubt she could hear Barbara the wood pigeon talking.

'I will leave a note,' announced Barbara's voice, 'and if they miss the dragon, there is nothing more we can do. We've tried for days now!'

Holly knew there was no time to waste; she shouted up the chimney, almost making herself hoarse with the effort.

'It's me, Holly! I'm here, I'm here! And what dragon?' she hollered.

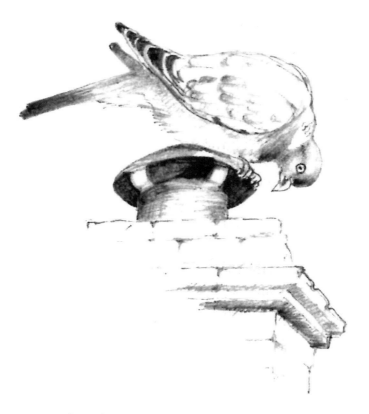

At first there was silence. Up above the chimneys, Barbara had heard the muffled sound of Holly's voice, and, cocking her tiny head to one side, listened intently.

At the bottom of the chimney and hearing no immediate reply, the girls thought they were too late.

But after a few seconds, they heard again the familiar cooing voice of Barbara drifting back down the chimney.

'Girls, at last! How wonderful! We have no time to lose - we came to tell you that our friend the Chinese Green Dragon will be visiting the magic garden tomorrow! He only comes to the garden once every five years and is quite magnificent; we didn't want you two to miss the chance of meeting him!'

Holly quickly relayed this information to Vikki, and they both lent up the chimney and shouted, 'We would love to come!'

The girls thought hard: tomorrow was a school day, and so that was that. Maybe after school, the dragon would still be in the garden - all they could do was hope.

The following day they raced home from school, arriving home quicker than ever and shocking their Mum, who was just starting to prepare dinner.

'You'll have to play outside for an hour or so!' said Mum.

'We're not very hungry – take your time!' they called back as they disappeared out of the back door, leaving their Mum staring quizzically after them. Usually they were very hungry after school!

As soon as the children reached the little narrow grass path that wound downwards towards the rose garden, they knew they were out of sight and sound of the house - and so they could begin to talk about the magnificent visitor who was about to come to the garden.

How big would it be and would it have wings? Would it breathe fire?

They chatted away until they were interrupted by a chirpy voice behind them.

'You're lucky the Chinese Green Dragon hasn't arrived yet!' And with that, Claudia, one of the red squirrels of the garden, gently climbed up Holly and sat on her shoulder with a cheeky grin.

Barry, the other red squirrel, quickly followed suit and placed himself on Vikki's shoulder.

The two girls were thrilled! Firstly it was a relief to know that they had not missed the mysterious dragon, and secondly it was always so nice to chat to their squirrel friends as they walked along, and to stroke their bushy red tails.

Within a few moments, all four of them had arrived at the tall cedar tree; and saw, sheltered beneath its large floppy branches, lots of the other animals from the garden sitting patiently waiting. They were thrilled when they spotted Mr Leafblower, who was entertaining a group of grey fluffy rabbits by doing his funny little dance - he did look silly!

Feeling something tug at her sleeve, Vikki bent down and was pleased to see Sooty. Sooty was the little black poodle from next door who was now also a regular visitor to the magic garden too; Vikki bent down and patted his short curly black coat.

'What fun!' Sooty said, wagging his tail furiously from overexcitement. 'I'm going to talk to the Green Dragon!'

'Oh do be careful, Sooty,' said Vikki, 'you don't want to get into any trouble. Do wait until you're introduced properly or the Dragon might not like it!'

Sooty was now scooting round and round chasing his tail. Vikki new full well that this was a sign that he was too excited to have listened to what she said! They would need to keep an eye on him when the Chinese Dragon arrived, because sometimes Sooty could be naughty.

'Do you think he will speak Chinese only or will we be able to understand him?' a breathless Sooty called out to the girls, as he darted this way and that.

Mr Leafblower, having finished his dance, now joined the little group of friends and, with a big beaming smile, sat down beside them. He always wore a jacket and trousers made of leaves, and was actually smaller than the children but much rounder.

Everyone began to talk at once as the group multiplied. After they had caught up on each other's news, they settled down again, and Mr Leafblower's voice rang out as he began to tell them everything he knew about the Dragon.

'Our friend the Magnificent,' then after a long pause he said, 'Dragon!' and went on to tell them all he knew about the green visitor.

He had a funny way of speaking - pausing between words at the wrong place and then booming on as if making a grand speech, which always made the girls smile. They adored their friend and his quirky ways.

Mr Leafblower explained that the Chinese Green Dragon really was everything they thought a dragon would be - but most astonishing of all, he told them that the Dragon also came from a **magic garden** similar to their own!

Holly and Vikki were immediately filled with questions. Another magic garden? How was this possible? And, Vikki wondered privately, would a real Dragon still blow out fire?

As abruptly as he had started, Mr Leafblower sat down and was completely silent - stopping, it seemed, in mid sentence as he always did.

All at once things began to change. It didn't exactly get dark, but greener - a pale, misty green that swirled around and engulfed them all like smoke. Then the green fog began to take shape, and got denser and denser until it formed into a long curling body that seemed to have no end.

As it settled, it covered all of the garden, twirling around the trees. Every now and then it went up and down, forming a tunnel of tail which they found they could easily walk under - and which they did just for fun!

'Hurry!' said Monty, disappearing around the edge of one of the garden walls and following the route laid out by the dragon's tail.

The girls were stunned by the incredible length of this beast. As they walked faster and faster to keep up with Monty, Vikki broke the silence and said, 'Is this its tail or its body?'

It was Sooty who replied, firmly, 'Definitely body and not tail, otherwise it would wag!'

'I wonder where on earth its head is!' Vikki said, choosing to ignore Sooty who she knew was just being ridiculous. At least, she hoped he was, because a wagging dragon's tail could be very tricky!

After what felt like at least a one mile walk around the greenish haze, they finally caught sight of two flapping wings, each about a metre long. After following the long, caterpillar-like tail for so long, they had got quite used to it - rather forgetting that of course there was much more to the rest of this marvellous creature.

Victoria felt butterflies flapping about in her tummy as she took it all in. A little in front of the wings, she could now see the back of an enormously broad, square-shaped head, belonging to a rather handsome and grand Chinese Dragon. His body was covered with emerald green scales which shimmered in the sunlight. The girls stared, open-mouthed, hardly able to believe they were standing right beside a real live dragon!

Monty now introduced them all to the dragon, whose name, by the way, was Ian. The girls privately thought that this didn't sound very Chinese at all, but considered it might be impolite to say so. Vikki gave Ian a speechless smile, finding that she loved him at once, and managed to eventually reply with a friendly 'hello.'

The dragon turned his large yellow eyes towards the two dainty little girls in front of him and asked in a crackly voice, 'May I offer you some of my fine jasmine tea and mooncakes?'

Feeling brave, Holly moved towards the dragon nervously, and asked him only slightly hesitantly to explain what a mooncake was. She was actually a little hungry, and certainly intrigued to know more.

The dragon's roar caught everyone off guard, for it was the loudest thing most of the garden's inhabitants had ever heard. Strangely, though, it was not scary - this roar was a dragon roaring with laughter at the funny two-legged little girl he saw beside him! He could not believe she had not tasted mooncakes, and said between his peals of laughter that she absolutely must today.

He was so taken with the children that he invited them to climb up onto his back, while he explained that mooncakes were in fact what she might know as fortune cookies. They had two main components: something nice to eat a bit like a biscuit, and something to tell.

Just then, from the wings of the dragon, two miniature men appeared wearing conical hats with trays carrying beautiful china cups and teapots. These men quickly served them some refreshing jasmine tea - and, best of all, the children were each given a fortune cookie, or a 'mooncake', as were all the other animals.

Then, walking effortlessly backwards, the two Chinese men disappeared again through a little flap under the dragon's wing.

As the girls enjoyed their mooncakes, Monty casually jumped up onto the dragon's head to the girls' surprise and began to scratch it! This was greeted, somewhat surprisingly, with much appreciation by the dragon, who appeared very happy to be groomed in this way.

The Dragon then began to tell them all about China and the magic garden he lived in, and how similar it was to theirs.

Just like Firwood, it appears that a tiny fragment of moon had dropped down, causing all sorts of magical effects. Like Monty at Firwood, the Chinese Dragon was the guardian of the special Chinese garden and all of its inhabitants. His garden was situated on the banks of the Yangtze river, and it was the only other magic garden apart from Firwood in the whole world.

Ian is a very relaxed Dragon, breathing only smoke and not fire, thought Vikki, as she listened dreamily while he told them more about his magic garden and about all of his favourite things. These included bathing in hot springs, chewing on bamboo, and visiting his panda friends who lived in Japan.

After this, the two guardians of the magic gardens fell into a deep and obviously private conversation, so the girls and the other animal friends happily unravelled the messages within their mooncakes and finished the delicious jasmine tea.

Although most of the fortune cookies were quite vague, with messages to be careful or alluding to good fortune to come, one was quite specific. Strangely enough, this was found inside the mooncake belonging to Sooty. Sooty read his out in a cheerful clear voice, as he was now very adept at switching from barking to talking when in the magic garden.

'Not north, not south, nor east but west
You will lead and guide the rest
They with little strength remaining
Run from ever blackness gaining
In the darkness light will pour
An enemy will share a door
what will be was always meant
The good will rise the bad are spent'

'Oooh!' said the twin squirrels - and immediately, lots of ideas of what this could mean were bandied about. Nothing could be settled upon, however, and the animals and children were left wondering. Little did they know that they would all find out soon enough!

Amongst all of this chaotic chatter, a flash of green and gold light caught all of their attention. Before they all knew it, the dragon was gone - quite literally in a flash!

'He's not one for goodbyes,' Monty shouted across to the children with a smile on his face.

'You're not kidding!' said a wide-eyed Sooty, who was still rereading the message he had found inside his fortune cookie.

Walking with them back towards the house, Monty was very quiet and seemed deep in thought, if not a little anxious. So it was no surprise when he told them that the dragon had brought some disturbing news. He would explain properly next time they met, as it was already getting late and time for the children to go home.

'For now,' he said, 'I have work to do and must speak with the Blue Treeglies.'

And with that, he bounded past the house and down to the front lawn. The girls caught the uneasiness in his voice.

However, they also suddenly realised how late home they were!

Chapter Two

The Return of the Evil Thworgs

Now tucked up in bed, the girls whispered quietly to each other about the dragon and how exciting it had been to meet him - but what Monty could have meant when he spoke of disturbing news? They were very keen to talk again with him and find out just what was going on.

'Why would Monty need to talk to the Blue Treeglies? It must be very important!' Vikki whispered to her sister.

Both girls had been lucky enough to see these strange crescent moons of blue light that occasionally glided around the garden. They didn't quite know what to make of them, but remembered that Monty had explained that the Treeglies were the good spirits of the garden.

Most importantly, however, they remembered how

the Blue Treeglies had once breathed life back into the fallen hedgehogs and saved their lives, in one of their previous adventures in the magic garden.

So whatever was going on, if the Blue Treeglies were involved it must be something very important. And they must find out tomorrow as soon as possible!

Waking late the next morning, Holly had momentarily forgotten the adventures of the night before. Sunlight poured in through the window beside her bed, warming her cheek and promising a perfect day ahead. Then, all at once, she remembered everything that had happened yesterday and ran to see if her sister was out of bed, which she was!

Both girls agreed with each other that Monty had seemed upset with what Ian the dragon had told him, prompting them to head off into the garden to look for him and find out why.

They found him by the entrance to Mr Leafblower's house, which was actually the compost heap at the back of the garden. Cinnamon and Treacle, the two long-haired guinea pigs, were also there.

Seeing the girls approach, Mr Leafblower boomed: 'Come inside, come inside!'

Smiling brightly at the girls, he turned around and used his strong back legs to kick away a pile of roots and twigs from the back of the compost heap. Doing this, he revealed the small door to his wonderful den.

Mr Leafblower's den was accessed down a sturdy metal ladder which they easily climbed down, and it was lit with car headlights dotted around the floor. At the bottom there were two old but comfortable sofas, and a variety of easy chairs. These, he informed them, he had found and retrieved from certain destruction - at least two had been headed for the local tip, he asserted, opening his eyes and arms wide with incredulity.

'Humans,' he said - then, after a long pause, continued, 'do not fully understand recycling.' With this, he plonked down on a chair which Holly was sure she recognised! It was very worn and a little of the stuffing was sticking out of the left side, where a big tear had appeared in the frayed purple flowery material.

When they were all seated, the girls, unable to wait any longer, asked Monty to explain about the 'disturbing news' brought by the dragon and why he had been so worried.

And here, sitting comfortably on the recycled seating in Mr Leafblower's den, they learnt about the plight of the Sheponies of Rowan Hill - not realising at the time how much this would affect both them and the magic garden.

Monty began: 'Sheponies are like mini Shetland ponies, different to these relatives mainly because they are much smaller, standing only about thirty centimetres high. They are equally known for their determination, intelligence and kindness. Thousands of years ago, a tiny group settled in the Welsh hills.'

'Gosh, they sound even smaller than Sooty!' Holly murmured, attempting to picture in her mind ponies that could be so small.

'Sheponies have lived peacefully, grazing and foraging in the Welsh mountains, undisturbed for a very long time,' Monty continued.

'In fact' he said, anticipating the next question, 'they have never ever been seen by any humans and have always been very careful to remain hidden from them;

23

they are a timid and private breed. Their existence is, however, known to other animals, but still they prefer to stay close to the herd keeping to themselves which the other animals respect.'

Actually that was just what Victoria was about to ask! For surely if anyone had seen such wonderful creatures they would have heard about it.

'The Sheponies do have some special friends though,' Monty said, 'they have had a long association with the tiny stick people who live in the trees, who have even been seen riding the little ponies. This is, of course, a great honour.'

The girls smiled at each other as they heard mention of the tiny stick people, for they too were their friends. These tiny people made of twigs lived high in the branches of the fir trees in the magic garden, and the girls were always thrilled if they got chance to play with them. How funny it would be to see them riding tiny ponies!

'However-'

And at this point Monty's fur stood on end. By the look on his face, the girls guessed that what he was about to tell them might be quite upsetting. But they were even more shocked than they could have imagined as he informed the children of the very worst possible news.

'Thworgs have driven the Sheponies out of their hills.'

Heaving a sigh, Monty carried on, 'Worse still, it seems that whilst trying to protect their homeland, many have been hurt.'

Monty's head dropped low as he delivered this piece of information; he himself clearly found it distressing. With newfound anger, he relayed what the Chinese Dragon had told him the day before.

As he flew high over Rowan Hill, the Dragon could not see any sign of the little herd he was used to seeing at this very spot; also, sensing great distress with his incredible dragon senses, he became concerned. He and the Sheponies had known each other for over a thousand years, and he suspected at once that something was terribly wrong.

A flock of swans had caught his eye and beckoned to him; flying alongside him they told him that they, too, were concerned for the ponies. Normally they would see at least some of them grazing.

Even stranger, earlier that day they had seen dark floating shapes in the sky above where the ponies usually were. The swans could not identify what the beings were but were sure they were not of animal type. The temperature on Rowan Hill had also dropped suddenly, freezing a nearby pond that they would normally drink from.

This was grave news indeed. Thanking the swans, Ian flew lower and back again over the hill.

He encountered everything confirming what the swans had told him. And then, a thousand feet below his own flight path, Ian spotted a vast number of these dark 'beings' hovering. Horrified, he immediately recognised that these were the evil entities the creatures of magic gardens across the world called Thworgs!

Knowing them as old enemies of all living creatures, he felt a sense of dread. Their presence here at Rowan Hill could have no good attached to it.

A dragon in full flight could not easily drop down through the clouds unseen to investigate, and so he knew he must remain cautious. All he could know for certain was that the little ponies were in danger. If he could somehow hinder Thworgs, he would!

And with that thought in mind, he craned his neck back and blew towards the wood at the bottom of the hill, where he was sure the Sheponies would seek refuge if they needed to. A mist of thick green dragon smoke which would confuse the Thworgs' senses and help hide the ponies' whereabouts, until he had chance to talk with Monty.

Before reaching the magic garden of Firwood, Ian once again had received news of the herd from a fine white swan sent to find him. The evil Thworgs had already attacked the ponies and taken their land; those left had sought shelter in a nearby wood.

Monty heaved a sigh as he delivered to his friends this final piece of heart-breaking news.

'The rest of the herd escaped by fleeing down a narrow rocky path that led to a small wood of Rowan trees, where they are now sheltering about twenty miles west of here.'

Holly could hardly believe what she had heard. She felt so angry; it wasn't the first time she had heard about the evil Thworgs.

The Thworgs had spent many years trying to find out the location of their own magic garden, so that they could steal the sacred moonpiece that was buried there. Their only purpose was to steal the moonpiece and to destroy the magic garden; they could not bear to see beauty and happiness and were cold, heartless beings. They were already the sworn enemies of the residents of the magic garden.

At this point Mr Leafblower leapt to his feet, unable to contain his fury.

'What is to be-' and after a few moments, he

continued, 'done?' very loudly.

Cinnamon and Treacle squashed their little hairy bodies together for comfort, and sighed long whistling sighs as they digested this dreadful news.

Monty spoke quietly but firmly.

"The Sheponies need help; it will not be long before the dragon's green mist evaporates. Even as we speak, the Thworgs will be searching for the rest of the the herd, knowing they are now homeless and vulnerable. The Thworgs have taken their land and probably seek to capture these little horse-like creatures, who are naturally gentle and no match for such an enemy.

'However, there is a great danger in also trying to help them. For in doing so, we risk...'

With this, he took a deep breath and continued, '...the discovery of the magic garden itself, and perhaps our own downfall.

'This decision must be made by all who live in the magic garden for it will have far-reaching consequences. Though I am privileged to be the cat-guardian of this place, it would be wrong of me not to seek the opinion of all who live here, on such a grave matter as this.'

The full weight of what Monty had said fell upon the little group gathered underground in Mr Leafblower's den. Everyone was momentarily silent while they absorbed the seriousness of the situation.

Having given everyone a little time to take it all in, Monty once again addressed his friends.

'I believe there is only one course of action. We must find the remaining Sheponies and offer our help. We cannot abandon our friends.' And lifting his head high with all the presence of a leader, he stood before them and asked them to join him in this dangerous quest. For without the help of all the animals, Monty knew it would be impossible to save the Sheponies.

At once all those present agreed, for they were united in their love for all good animals, and their belief in the rights of all animals who might be targeted by the evil, hateful Thworgs.

'I have already spoken with the Blue Treeglies and will call a meeting for the rest of the inhabitants of the garden this evening. Holly and Victoria - I need your help to bring Sooty the poodle, for I suspect we may need him.'

It was just after dusk when Monty informed all those who lived in the magic garden of what had happened to the Sheponies of Rowan Hill.

The tiny stick people had tumbled down from the branches of the fir trees where they lived and were clearly saddened by what they heard. Stepping forward, they assured him that they were more than willing to help however they could. Adamant and keen, they left no one in doubt that they were to be included in any rescue plan.

Monty thanked them; this would be very useful and very necessary, because the stick people were great friends of the Sheponies and had their trust.

The stick people, who were quite tiny, were also known to have amongst them fine horsemen and women who could be needed to ride the little ponies to safety.

As the evening air got colder, Monty began answering questions and calming the animals, for they were rightly outraged and a little scared by what they heard had happened to their Shepony friends. They knew that the

Thworgs also sought the magic garden, and that they could easily be next.

Among this commotion, Holly felt something tickle her arm - and looking down, she was thrilled to see that her tiny stick friends had come to say hello and had begun to climb onto her lap. As usual, she held out her hand and one of the little stick girls in a gorgeous bluebell dress spun around on her palm and showed her a little dance. It felt nice to be with them tonight and Holly forgot for a moment the purpose of the meeting. She watched in awe as the stick people showed her their many tricks of juggling and dancing, which they always loved to do, because they were terrible show-offs - but in a very sweet way!

Everyone in the garden was unanimous. Even though the risk to the garden could not be underestimated, and they knew that if the Thworgs found its location, they would be fighting for their own existence, the ponies were in grave danger, hiding alone and afraid in their small wood of rowan trees. The animals of the magic garden knew that they must do something, and so a plan was hatched to try to save the Sheponies right there and then.

It was hard for Holly and Victoria to get to sleep that night, with the thought of the little animals hiding alone in the dark and not knowing what would happen to them. At least they could be sure that if anyone could lead a rescue, it would be their very own cat: Monty, the cat-guardian of Firwood.

Chapter Three

A Secret Journey

As luck would have it, tomorrow was Saturday so the children were off school.

It had been decided that Sooty, due to his incredible sense of smell, and twelve of the finest stick riders, would set out with Monty, Mr Leafblower, and the children on the first part of the long journey to find the Sheponies.

The girls would tell their parents they wanted to go on a bike ride and ask if they could take a picnic, which they were pretty sure Mum would agree too, as all parents love activities which involve fresh air and exercise!

Next, they would ask their neighbours if they could take Sooty along

with them - which was not unusual as the children often took the little dog for walks.

Mum said yes to the picnic and Holly let out a

sigh of relief. But before they even mentioned Sooty their mother went on to inform the children that the neighbours were going away for the whole weekend.

Vikki gasped loudly, realising that much of their rescue plan depended on the little poodle and his strong sense of smell. What on earth would they do without him?

But she needn't have worried, for Mum carried on: 'So, girls, I have said that we will look after Sooty all weekend, and I am expecting you two to walk him both days.'

Holly and Victoria were jubilant and both responded to this a little too enthusiastically, causing their Mum to wonder aloud: 'Now just what are you two up to?'

Holly quickly took control of the situation and answered more calmly, 'Oh, Mum, you know how much we love Sooty. Can we go and get him now?'

Glancing up at the kitchen clock, Mum said yes and handed them the spare key to the neighbours' house.

What their parents didn't know, nor his owners, was that Sooty had already enjoyed many adventures in the magic garden. He had found it great fun the first time he had accidentally hopped over the garden wall and found that, while in Firwood, he could actually talk!

He had even been in Mr Leafblower's den and ridden on his Leaf Flume, and had often careered around the garden with lots of little stick people riding on his back, demonstrating the stick people's great horsemanship - or, rather, dogmanship!

This adventure, however, would be different. The girls knew that Sooty wouldn't be tucked up at home after playing all day with them like their parents thought. Instead of lapping up the fresh water that they would put down for him with his favourite food, he would be hiding in a field with Monty, probably scared and certainly hungry.

How lucky they all felt that the first part of the plan was executed perfectly. With a picnic in hand and Sooty wagging his tail in buoyant mood, they fetched their bikes from the shed in the back of the garden, carefully avoiding the tall nettles that had grown around its edges.

Monty now reminded everyone that they would not be able to talk with the children once they had left the garden for this power of speech between them would be gone.

The children knew they could transport the others quickly using their bicycles. Time was truly of the essence, and the other animals needed to conserve their strength for the last part of the journey.

Sooty sat in the basket at the front of Holly's bike and Monty in her back pack - it did look rather odd!

However, nowhere near as odd as Mr Leafblower, who sat tucked in behind Vikki on her bicycle, wearing Vikki's pale blue cagoule with the hood pulled up over his head to hide him. No one outside the garden would have seen anyone quite like Mr Leafblower! Even though it was a very serious task that they were about to undertake, they did all laugh when they saw the way he looked.

The tiny stick riders, who always took such pride in their clothes, came prepared. They wore dark green riding trousers, finely woven from nettle leaves that were tucked inside smart red velvety foxglove boots. Clinging to the bars of the bikes, they were held safe by strong ivy vines cut last night in the garden.

The long journey began, and the girls did their very best to cycle as fast and as far as they could along the road that headed west, guided by the keen eyes of Michelle and Barbara the wood pigeons, who flew just ahead and above them.

Vikki could feel her legs tiring as they kept peddling mile after mile in the heat of the day, but she didn't complain or even ask to rest.

Holly, who cycled just ahead of her, kept checking back over her shoulder. She could see the tired look on her sister's face and was proud of her effort, but she knew that they still must press on and they did.

The weight of their companions slowed them down and it was nearly noon when they finally reached their destination - they had been cycling for well over two hours.

At a wooden gate, the entrance to a field of foot high green corn, they completed the first part of the journey. Holly and Vikki were glad to rest their legs by the post that Barbara and Michelle were perched upon.

This was as far as the girls could take their friends. The others must proceed on foot across the fields that gradually led upwards to the small wood of rowan trees. At least they were still fresh and had plenty of energy for the next part of the journey which they hoped they could make before nightfall.

Hugging their friends and waving goodbye, the girls were now left tired and hungry. They had left their picnic with the others who would need it later; turning their bikes around, they headed back to Firwood, with Michelle the wood pigeon on hand to guide them back to the safety of the magic garden.

Vikki wiped a tear from her face and bit her lip as she peddled home, wondering if they would ever see their friends again. She thought about Sooty and how silly he could be and how cross he sometimes made them - and then how much she adored him! What a big task for such a little dog! And how willing and brave he had been to help!

The girls were so tired and despondent when they got home that their parents wondered if they had been arguing. And though they briefly spoke about the day's events to each other, they really couldn't be bothered to talk at all because they needed more than anything rest and a good night's sleep. They knew that tomorrow Barbara would fly back to the garden if she could and bring news - all they could do was wait.

On Sunday morning, the girls were subdued, even when their parents said that their friend Tom was coming to play.

Then Dad reminded them, 'Don't forget to walk

Sooty again this morning!'

Stiffening at this reminder, for they did not like to hide things from their parents, the girls headed off to their neighbours' house, knowing full well that Sooty was not there!

Everything had happened so quickly that this part of the plan - keeping Sooty's absence secret - had not been thought about, and had to be improvised now.

After using the spare key to enter the neighbours' house, the two girls sat briefly down at the kitchen table. Holly was swinging her legs and Vikki was day dreaming.

'Holly, do you remember when we had to pretend that Tom was coming in for lunch, even though he had been shrunk to the size of a pea?' Vikki said.

The girls now looked at each other and they knew immediately they must confide in their friend Tom. Tom had shared previous adventures with them in the garden and knew Mr Leafblower and the others, and would never forgive them if they didn't tell him. More importantly, he might be able to help!

So it was a relief when they walked back up the drive that they saw him waving to them. They ran up to meet him and explain everything that had happened. We walked Sooty, Holly called into the open door to her parents as she passed it.

*   *   *   *

As soon as Mr Leafblower, Monty, Sooty and the stick people had alighted from the bikes, they began their long walk towards the wood.

The tiny stick people divided themselves between their three companions. The sun was high and only a few fluffy white clouds interrupted the pale blue sky. The heat of the day made the march harder - but just when it was getting to be unbearable, especially for Sooty and Monty (having their own built in body-warmer coats), a cool northerly breeze began to blow, for which they were grateful.

Stopping just after five o'clock, Mr Leafblower spread out the picnic kindly left by the girls on top of the blue cagoule that he had worn earlier. Barbara flew down and joined them with the excellent news that they had covered five miles - with luck they may even reach the ponies tonight!

Mr Leafblower unscrewed one of his bell-shaped bottles and poured the water from it into two little foil dishes that had previously held something humans liked to eat. As usual, he had found a good use for things that humans didn't think to recycle! He had tucked them in one of his many leaf pockets for an occasion just like this and was humming contentedly.

The water was gratefully lapped up by his four-legged friends; meanwhile, the stick people were prepared as ever with little satchels of redcurrants and dainty cupcakes in a rainbow of colours, which they offered generously to share with their much bigger friends.

Even though they had a dangerous mission ahead of them, this well-earned rest relieved the tension that all the animals had felt whilst on the move. For now they were a happy band of travellers, prompting a few somersaults and gymnastics from the tiny stick people: a performance that was guaranteed to lift spirits!

After an hour's rest, Monty asked the animals to get ready for what he hoped was the final part of the journey. From here on, they would rely on Sooty's keen sense of smell. With the possibility of Thworgs hovering close by, it was not safe for Barbara to fly anymore.

Wishing them good luck and promising to come back soon, she said farewell and headed home, careful not to show those she left behind the concern she felt. It would do no good to stir up anxious feelings.

Sooty wagged his tail with delight; he felt very special having been selected for his role and was determined to do it well. He waited patiently for the signal, which for a normally restless little dog was quite a feat! When Monty nodded towards him, for all the animals now knew they must be as quiet as possible, he sniffed the ground and began to lead the way.

For at least a mile, they continued on the slight incline of the field, following the little dog as he tried desperately to pick up any scent of the ponies. Monty was worried, and had begun to wonder if they had by any chance taken the wrong route; Sooty stopped and waited for the others to catch up.

It was harder going now, and steeper, as they had left the final field and were making their way up a slight hill. Here the ground was stubbly and uneven, and only trodden by goats and sheep adept at walking on such jagged land.

Mr Leafblower became quite breathless keeping up with Sooty. They were closely followed by Monty, who, whenever he could, shimmied up any lone tree or pile of rocks to check for the enemy.

'Onwards and upwards!' Mr Leafblower whispered encouragingly to the three stick riders he carried in his top three pockets. The stick people were carrying miniature arrows, the size of sewing needles but fashioned out of nettles, primed and ready as they scanned the countryside around them.

Then, just over the next rise, Sooty suddenly stopped. Following his signal, the others got down and crept slowly up to join him.

Sooty had sensed another presence, and it was not like anything else he had ever come across. In fact it made him shiver - there was a coldness in the air, just slight now and then carried by the wind. Putting his nose to the ground he could also pick up something else and he snuffled around this spot until he was absolutely sure. It was the scent of what he guessed must be a Shepony. Different to the familiar smell of Horse he knew, sharper but of a close relative he was sure of that and yes here it was again just a metre in front and stronger, a little pony had been here and not long ago!

This was the trail! And the wood must be very close by, even though it was not yet in sight, it must be just over the next ridge. Now he turned to his friends and told them what he had deduced with his clever nose. "Well done Sooty" Monty whispered and now speaking quietly but quickly, for he was mindful that the Sheponies had been alone in the wood for days now, he outlined what they must do next. Together they listened respectfully to their leader as he told them his plan.

First they must get to the wood and seek the head of the herd and explain they were here to help. It would be Monty who would carry them on his back to the outer trees of the wood.

Once in the branches of the trees the stick people could move at an incredible speed. They could swing from branch to branch, slip and slide down thick boughs and crucial to the success of this rescue plan be completely camouflaged from the enemy! Trees were their home and like fish in water no other creature no Thworgs could match them here. The stick people nodded smiling, for they had such a pleasant demeanour that nothing at all could make them unhappy or cross and they were always willing to help.

'You my friends must make contact with the Sheponies. They know and trust you and will be very glad of friendship in their terrible situation I am certain. You must find out the state of the little ponies, are any injured? How many remain in the wood? And make them understand that we mean them no harm and that we come from the magic garden and are here to help in any way we can'

The last light of the day now departed and the darkness sat like a veil around them, providing an extra benefit of cover to the little gang. It also meant it was time to go!

There was only one problem: Monty could not fit all of the riders on his back together. To do the journey twice would prove too dangerous - and so he asked the stick people if they were willing to be temporarily shrunk with the magic lupin dust that all those who lived in the garden knew so well! He always carried a small amount with him, just in case of emergencies like these.

Of course, the stick people readily agreed; the twelve stick riders now jumped to their feet and stood in line, each with a small hand outstretched. Unscrewing the top to a small jar, Monty carefully dabbed a speck of lupin dust, no bigger than a grain of salt, onto each of their tiny palms.

Within seconds, every one of the stick people had become miniature versions of themselves! However, the dust would only last an hour or so - and so they had to be quick.

Monty stood, and the stick people, quick as lightening, climbed his legs and sat in rows of three, holding onto little stick-handfuls of his tabby fur as if they were reins. All twelve could now comfortably ride together on the back of this brave cat.

It had already been decided that Mr Leafblower and Sooty would wait close by near some rocks that formed a little crag on the hillside, they would be safe their hidden by the blackness of nightfall. Monty once having deposited his precious load of stick riders, would with his keen cats eyes, search the immediate area around the wood for sight or sound of Thworgs. He would remain at the perimeter of the trees until the stick people returned with news. Returning to the crag he would rendezvous at midnight with Sooty and Mr Leafblower if he could, if not they must wait but only until noon the next day.

Then Monty made them promise that if he did not return by noon at the latest the next day that they must retrace their steps and head back home to the garden.

Monty did not say so but all present knew that this could mean that their mission had failed and that the garden may have lost its brave cat-guardian and the twelve finest stick warriors ever.

Sooty's tail dropped and for the first time he felt very frightened. Mr Leafblower lifted Sooty onto his knee and stroked the little dog telling him not to worry and encouraged him to get some sleep while he could.

"Soon my little (long pause) friend you will need that smart nose of yours to get us all" and finally he said "home".

With a quick farewell Monty was off at speed ducking and weaving his way up towards the ridge and sure enough as soon as he reached it he saw about five metres ahead of him the wood!

The next part of the journey would be the most dangerous; now the land panned out flat towards the wood and provided no camouflage.

Monty was sure that this would be the time that if the Thworgs were indeed here, they would strike. He was fearful for his little companions and could only hope that the green mist that their friend the Dragon had blown days earlier had indeed worked and he and the stick riders had got here first.

Dropping down Monty crept along the ground that led towards the wood, as he got closer he could hear the whooshing of the leaves in the trees as they moved in the evening breeze.

A sudden noise to the right made him cower and he flattened himself into the ground. With all of his senses on red alert, he was relieved that at least as yet he could not feel the ice cold chill of Thworgs. Unless.... but Monty did not let this train of thought continue, he must focus on the job in hand – he must reach the safety of the trees!

Only two metres to go and they would be safe and with this thought in mind Monty sprung- fast forward, feeling his fur gripped even tighter as he did so by twelve sets of tiny hands, and he reached the trunk of the first rowan tree in six leaps of a cats legs.

He did not stop until he had scrambled up it, within seconds his riders had dismounted and effortlessly disappeared into leafy branches, determined to play their part in the plan and find their pony friends.

Very soon they would return to their normal size and head off into the trees without him.

Chapter Four

Lost Sheponies

Monty padded quietly around the outer trees of the wood, at home with the sight and sounds of the night.

Glancing up at a three-quarter moon high above the trees, he did not feel entirely alone. The moon was once home to the tiny fragment - the moon-piece - that was held in the garden and gave it its magic, even the ability to speak like a human to the animals' human friends! And his mind cast warmly back to Holly and Victoria, and the help they had given the animals in the past few days.

A high note now pierced the silence only once, and he recognised the trill sound of the horn used by the stick people, signalling to him that they had made contact with the Sheponies.

Such was his relief, and knowing they would need time to talk, he lay his exhausted body down in some bracken and slept, his ears still pricked in case of attack.

Woken by touch not sound, Monty was careful to remain completely still.

Aware of the intruder, he prepared himself for trouble. He half-opened one of his eyes - whatever it was, it was already crawling on him, and he was already too late!

His mind raced as he quickly ran through the options left to him. Luckily, however, he did not need to leap immediately into action. He almost laughed out loud when he heard a familiar voice and realised it was two of the stick people, for they alone could successfully creep up on a snoozing cat!

'Come, come with us, you shall see, you shall see!' they now hummed and sang in their sugary voices, tugging at his fur with their little hands.

Monty followed his friends, who were zigzagging from branch to branch, further into the wood. Here the trees thickened and closed in together; it got darker as the light was held out by the vast branches.

Just as he began to wonder how on earth anything bigger than a cat could pass this way, the trees began to thin in number and melt away.

Eventually they opened out again on all sides, forming a clearing which was surrounded neatly by particularly tall straight trees like soldiers standing on guard. And then Monty heard a rustle, and, looking over towards its source, seeing at once, right in front of him, the most wonderful sight.

A herd of tiny ponies not much bigger than himself were gathered in the clearing! He could not tell how many – maybe a hundred, he guessed. Most had now turned to look at him.

The ponies all had glossy thick coats: some black and some dapple grey; and he noticed that there were several white ponies amongst the herd and chestnut brown ones too! They were quite breathtaking. They all had the same remarkable eyes: enormous and sky blue, which sparkled like diamonds and were framed by thick long lashes blinking gently as they gazed back towards him. Of all the creatures Monty had ever seen, these were quite the loveliest.

Trotting gracefully towards him, swishing her long

white tail, came the only piebald pony of the entire herd. Her head and body were a mixture of black white. She was very petite but perfectly formed, and as she approached Monty, Monty realised that these little ponies were only inches taller than himself.

Poppelana introduced herself as the leader of the herd, and pawed the ground three times with her right hoof then bucking her legs in the traditional Shepony greeting. Monty was not alarmed; his stick friends had forewarned him that a Shepony greeting could be a little scary!

Then Poppelana spoke: 'We shall all be friends together!' -and a gentle whinnying of little ponies rang out in the clearing as Monty was given the most valuable gift of all by the Sheponies of Rowan Hill: the gift of friendship.

Monty was touched; he knew from legend that an offer of friendship like this was very rarely given from a Shepony, and that he had been greatly honoured. No matter what passed in the future, these loyal friends would stand with him against any foe.

The stick people had told the ponies that the animals and children of Firwood had come to help them, and that Monty was their leader.

Now the two leaders of very different groups - Monty and Poppelana - must talk hastily, as they both knew that the threat of the Thworgs was greater with every passing minute. The evil Thworgs would soon move their search to a different area, inevitably finding the clearing and endangering the Sheponies once more.

It was time to decide what must be done! Poppelana sat now with her new friend Monty and shared with him the frightening events that had recently taken place.

As Ian the Chinese Dragon had suspected, the tiny ponies had been attacked by Thworgs and had had to flee from their home on Rowan Hill. The ponies had fought bravely but, being no match for such dark chilling beings, eventually had found a sad refuge in the wood close by.

At least most of them had.

And now Monty listened whilst Poppelana's voice grew heavy with emotion and she described to him exactly what had happened.

The ponies had, as usual, enjoyed the grass that grew plentiful on their hill that morning, the younger ones running and playing. Before they understood what was happening, darkness had filled the sky above them. What at first had looked like a flock of black birds then stopped and hung like a menacing throng of blackness above them.

'Everything happened so quickly,' Poppelana said in her warm, shy voice and continued her story.

Sensing danger, she signalled the herd to her - but just as she did so, they were attacked. She saw these strange black bodies move closer. They had long bent beaks like heads without features; their long bodies like thick smoke trailed beneath them.

'These dreadful beings brought an immense icy vapour with them, chilling the ground we stood upon. I realised now that they meant only harm, and at once they began to swoop and attack my family.'

Monty winced as he listened to the ordeal the little ponies had faced, and Poppelana continued.

Shocked at such an unprovoked attack, the ponies at first tried to fight off this unknown enemy. But the dark beings unleashed a sting of ice that pierced the soft skin of several of the herd, knocking them cruelly to the ground.

The herd now panicked and became disoriented, running in circles in an attempt to escape from the

Thworgs. They charged at the dark things, trying to protect their fallen brothers and sisters - but the swooping Thworgs attacked again and again, and their deathly chill drove the ponies back.

A deep hum had rang out across the hill, as the Thworgs spoke in one joined voice.

'This hill is now our hill,' it droned, repeating endlessly. 'This hill is now our hill. This hill is now our hill.'

Their purpose had become immediately clear: the Thworgs had come to claim the land of the Sheponies and keep it for themselves.

Bravely, the ponies who had escaped had tried once again to free their stricken relatives - but the chill of the Thworgs formed a barrier which they could not penetrate.

Forced to consider the safety of the rest of the herd, Poppelana made the most difficult decision she had ever had to make. The remaining herd must leave the hill the Sheponies had called home for six hundred years - and some of their friends behind them.

Reluctantly, she had ordered them away from their homeland to the wood near the bottom of the hill, where for a while they could be safe.

Poppelana flicked her ears as she remembered these terrible events. She could still hear in her mind the sound of the ponies' hooves clattering the hard earth as they fled and were still pursued by more Thworgs flying above them.

Monty was shocked by what he heard had happened. An angry light entered his eyes as he considered the injustice of the attack and the badness of Thworgs.

Poppelana carried on: 'Fourteen Sheponies were caught by the stinging chill the Thworgs unleashed. Our dear friends the swans have since told us that they are held tightly tied by their hooves at the top of the hill.'

A tremor rippled through her coat, highlighting the distress she felt, but she forced herself to go on.

'It was the swans who assured me that these evil things were indeed those known as Thworgs. I had heard about them , but never, ever did I believe that they would come to Rowan Hill and dare to take our land.'

Poppelana cast her eye protectively across her remaining herd and then continued.

'Just as it seemed we would all share the same fate, I felt the heat of a westerly wind blowing down and the Thworgs felt it too. They began to disperse, seemingly panicked by the heat and something above them.

'Green mist that dropped like a veil gave us the cover we needed and the time to get safely to the wood.'

Now facing an audience of these gentle elegant creatures, Monty was able to tell them that it had in fact been Ian the green dragon that had passed by and played this crucial part in the ponies' escape.

'It was the warmth of his breath and the green mist he blew that you saw and felt that day.'

The band of ponies whinnied and stamped as they acknowledged the gratitude they owed the dragon.

'Monty.' Poppelana now stood up beside him, only inches taller than her new friend; she was able to look directly into his sharp green eyes.

Arching her head back towards Rowan Hill she said, her voice calm but resolute, 'I intend to free my captured family. I cannot leave here without them. Although we despair about leaving this land, we can find and make a new home. But I will not leave any Sheponies here to suffer at the hands of these evil beings.'

Before anything else was said, Popellana moved swiftly, pressing her ear to the ground. She whispered as she did so that something or someone was approaching the clearing.

A cold air spread through the trees like the tendrils of a plant reaching out and searching. Then it was gone. A shiver ran through the herd. No more could they delay; the Thworgs were getting close.

Monty was suddenly aware that the merest drops of sunlight had started to dapple the leaves of the surrounding trees. It was dawn. Time was indeed running out, and to make matters worse, the cover of darkness was now gone.

Chapter Five

A Strange New Friend

Monty had not returned, nor had Sooty or Mr Leafblower had any news. A slice of the sun appeared on the horizon as dawn had begun to break. At least the two friends were both refreshed, and given their circumstances, had slept well nestled into a crag on the little hillside.

Mr Leafblower and Sooty could only hope that Monty was now with the Sheponies. They too had heard the one, shrill note that rang out in the night; and recognising at once the horn of their friends the stick people, they were hopeful of seeing the animals of the garden and the Sheponies soon.

Now they must wait. Surely Monty and the ponies would reach them by the deadline of noon.

Having given his word to Monty that he and Sooty would go back to the magic garden if nobody had reached them by then, Mr Leafblower began to place a little stone beside him as each hour passed so as to keep track of the time. His jolly nature meant that not once did he suspect they would not make it.

Sooty continued to sniff the air for any scent of the travellers, determined to lead them brilliantly down the hill and home. The little dog was restless and so now and then he crawled further up the hill in case he could catch the slightest hint of his friends on their way back. He was quite excited to meet these miniature horses that would be no taller than himself. Surely they could run faster than he could... and they would play such incredible games of chase!

Picturing this in his mind's eye, Sooty's tail began to wag involuntarily, and this caused Mr Leafblower to at least twice jump to his feet thinking Sooty had actually picked up the scent of their returning friends!

It was now almost noon, and Mr Leafblower hardly dared to catch the eye of Sooty. He knew he must insist soon that they walk back down the hill, beginning the journey home to the magic garden without the others. Not knowing what had befallen their friends would make this a very sad walk indeed.

The sun now directly above them like a big yellow sunflower announced it was noon. Reluctantly, Mr

Leafblower added the final pebble to his pile and began
to pack up.

Sooty sat down stubbornly. 'We cannot leave them!'
he said as firmly as a little puppy possibly could.

His friend patted him, admiring his courage.
'Unfortunately, my little companion, we must do as Monty
asked us to do. As the guardian of the Magic Garden,
it would be wrong to disobey his (pause) instructions.
Remember, we must protect the Magic Garden at all--'
and, holding his hand up as he usually did, he finished
by saying '--costs.'

Knowing this to be correct, and hardly noticing
Mr Leafblower's characteristically strange pauses, Sooty
joined his friend, his tail down. They had let noon slip
by, but now really must leave; and with heavy hearts they
began to retrace their steps downwards towards home.
They walked close to the hedgerow of trees that were
entwined with blackberry and other bushes whenever
possible, to keep themselves hidden.

They had only gone a mile or so when Sooty stopped
abruptly. His little stomach lurched as he saw something
he had seen before, and had hoped he would never see
again as long as he lived!

A round, green ball the size of a football now blocked
their path. It was asleep and snoring loudly! Luckily for

Sooty, this time there was only one. He immediately began to growl - he remembered his last encounter with the angry Greenlings who lived in one of tunnels that joined Mr Leafblower's den - and, of course, so did Mr Leafblower!

Not so long ago, Sooty had been kidnapped by these Greenlings because he had accidentally entered their tunnel without permission. They usually slept in a pile and were very grumpy if woken. To his cost, the little poodle had learnt that anything found in the Greenlings tunnel they kept - including him! A huge rescue had had to be mounted which was eventually successful, but it had been quite a scary adventure in Sooty's mind!

Unable to contain himself, Sooty ran at this new Greenling. Just as he did last time when he came face-to-face with them, he pulled at it with his teeth.

The Greenling woke at once and flicked out two small arms and legs and stared back at Sooty. And then it began to cry. Great dollops of tears poured from its eyes.

'Please don't eat me!' it gulped, facing the two companions.

For the first time in ages, Sooty and Mr Leafblower began to laugh. They laughed and laughed as they looked at the little green ball in front of them and thought how absurd it would be to eat it.

Then, coming to their senses and remembering that they were on an important mission, they forced themselves to stop.

This Greenling didn't look very angry at all, thought Sooty, and because he was really a soft-hearted and kind little dog, he lent forward and licked away one of its tears. At which point, the Greenling pulled back in his arms and legs and lay motionless in front of them, saying as he did so:

'So you **are** going to eat me!'

Mr Leafblower burst out laughing again!

'No, no......no!' said Mr Leafblower, pulling himself together and addressing the Greenling. 'Come come my little (long pause) fellow, dry those little green (pause) eyes, we mean you no harm!'

After quite a bit of coaxing, the little Greenling popped his arms and legs back out and listened to the funny man in front of him.

Mr Leafblower now introduced himself and Sooty and told him all about what had happened to the Sheponies and why they were now making their way back to the Magic Garden. Explaining about the Thworgs and their evil plans to steal magical land for themselves, he eventually finished by saying to the Greenling:

'So now perhaps you can see, we shoulder a great responsibility to return home.'

Then it was the turn of the little Greenling to tell his new friends how he had found himself alone in the field and lost.

Firstly he told them his name, which was Pinbean. Pinbean explained that although the Greenlings' tunnel began under the Magic Garden, it had many branches stretching for miles to the north, south, east, and west. Greenlings loved nothing more than extending their tunnels.

Mr Leafblower nodded knowingly; as a tunnel-dweller himself, he quite understood.

Moving quickly, the whole group of Greenlings had travelled along the west tunnel two days ago.

Three little Greenlings - Pinbean and two others -

had woken before the rest one morning. Being young and curious and quite naughty, they dug a hole up through the ground. A small flap of turfy grass made a tiny doorway out of the tunnel and into the field.

Because the doorway that they had made was so very small, they had to pull their last friend through with some effort, and the grass flap closed abruptly behind them, almost completely disguising the entrance.

Greenlings did not like to be in the daylight, and as soon as the little Greenlings had spent a few minutes outside, they decided to dash back into the tunnel.

But Pinbean had been distracted when a flock of ducks had flown above him. Having never seen ducks flying before, he stood gazing at them as they flew overhead. He was so amazed that he began to run along the field to keep up with the shadow they cast on the ground below. Of course he couldn't - and only when they were completely out of sight, he thought again about his friends, and getting back into the tunnel.

Turning his head from side to side, he couldn't see his friends; and then he started to panic and run around searching. But he was still unable to find the little flap of grass that was the door back into the tunnel. Now the field appeared huge in comparison to him, and the truth had dawned on him he was well and truly lost!

Once again, the little Greenling's eyes filled with pools of tears as he described to his new friends how he was now unable to find the grassy door. And how he had spent hours and hours searching until he was so exhausted he did what Greenlings did best: fall fast asleep.

'I will never see my mother and father and fifteen brothers and sixteen sisters again,' he said in a forlorn voice.

'Now, now, little--' and after an extremely long pause Mr Leafblower finished, '--Pinbean. We must get back to the garden and you will find your (pause) family. Yes, that's the only solution. It's settled then!' Mr Leafblower waved his hand theatrically. 'You will come with us! We would not leave you here lost and alone. My den beneath the compost heap has many tunnels, and we can easily find yours and then your family. You can even ride on my Leaf Flume!'

Pinbean was a little confused, but he could not bear to be alone anymore in a giant field and said decisively, 'Thank you!' He could not think of anything else to add and so he did a somersault, which made his new friends laugh again.

*   *   *   *

As they began to walk together down the hill, Sooty explained to Pinbean that Mr Leafblower's Leaf Flume was an amazing rollercoaster - probably the best in the whole world! It travelled at immense speed around enormous bends and loops! Sooty described all of this excitedly to his very unusual new friend - for who in the garden would believe that Sooty and a Greenling could ever be friends?

'Riding the Leaf Flume was actually how I ended up in your tunnel,' Sooty continued, and he recounted the whole story to Pinbean as they trudged along together.

What a funny sight they were making their way across the field: a Greenling, a little black poodle, and Mr Leafblower with his beaming smile and his ill-fitting jacket and trousers made of leaves. Nevertheless, they were all very glad to have each other for company and marched purposefully on, hoping to reach the Magic Garden before night fell.

And whenever the little Greenling tired, Sooty bent down and let him climb onto his back so that he could rest his small green legs a while.

Chapter Six

The Perilous Plan

Birdsong filled the wood, and the sun was now full and bright in the pale blue sky above the trees. The twelve stick people sat close to Poppelana and Monty, playing 'roll the beech nut' on a fallen tree trunk. As soon as Poppelana had finished telling Monty everything, they jumped spritely down.

The sudden chill that had travelled through the clearing had unsettled everyone. And now knowing that Monty too had all of the facts about the Thworgs and their actions, it was time to decide what must be done.

Efa, who led this small group of stick riders, now joined his cat-guardian and Shepony friends.

Together, the animals made a plan. The lives of many would depend upon their success, and there was a solemn air as the three of them talked. It was decided within minutes rather than hours, for time was against them and they knew they must act in haste, whether they liked it or not.

The first part of the plan was the most dangerous. The lives of many must be weighed against the lives of few. None of them took this lightly but accepted that it was inevitable in these circumstances.

An attempt would be made to rescue the ponies tied and held prisoner by the Thworgs on Rowan Hill. A knowledge of the shallow paths that skirted up the hill would provide an advantage against the enemy, and Poppelana was adamant she knew these paths more than anyone else. So it was agreed that this gentle creature would return to face her attackers.

She would not be alone, though. Efa and his people would ride on Poppelana's back, and dismount as close as they could to the prisoners. They would sneak silently between the stricken Sheponies. Using their incredibly strong and dexterous fingers usually used for sewing, carving and weaving nettle cloth, they would free the hooves of the little animals.

Efa stood, hands on stick hips, and told his friends confidently that such was their determination, these elected stick riders would be able to break the toughest knots ever tied by evil Thworgs!

Monty was thrilled by the bravery of these woodland people, but silently he prayed that they would not find their task made impossible by some ghastly device of the Thworgs that none of them had encountered before. The Thworgs were always inventing nasty ways to prevent good deeds being done.

An hour after Poppelana and her riders embarked on their climb back up the hill, it would be Monty's turn. He would lead the other 85 ponies to the edge of the wood. Even though it would still be daylight, he must take a chance and cross the few metres of open ground that he had covered a day earlier when he first found the wood.

This time he was headed home to the Magic Garden. Now he would have a herd of trusting miniature ponies to guide, and his judgement as to when to cross must be faultless. If they were attacked by Thworgs in the open - he shuddered at the thought - the consequences for these small creatures could be dire.

The final part of their plan was now explained to all. Presuming the crossing from the wood was successful, the herd would be led by Monty back across the grassy ground and across the fields towards the road.

Eventually, he would somehow get them back to the Magic Garden and to safety.

There was no time to work out exactly how, so he filed it to the back of his mind, concentrating instead on what the others would have to do.

Back on Rowan Hill, Poppelana would have deposited her crew of stick riders. Carefully, she would make her way around to the other side of the hill, which they calculated would take her the hour that Monty would wait. Once there, she would create a distraction, kicking the small rocks that in places littered the hillside and loosening them.

The three leaders glanced at each other; much would depend upon this downward avalanche of rocks and dust. Surely this would bring the enemy to investigate.

Listening and watching for this noise and dust would be Efa and his companions. As soon as the Thworgs sought to find the source of the disturbance, the stick people would move. This would be their best chance to free the captured little horses. They must find a way to untie them and ride them furiously down and away from the hill and their evil captors.

Efa and his people would each ride one of the ponies - they would ride like the wind, passing the wood, then turn, following the line of hedgerows down towards the lower field. Finally, they would walk to the edge of the cornfield that led to the road.

Here they might be lucky and meet with Monty and

the majority of the herd of Sheponies. If not, they too must find a way back to the magic garden led by Efa.

No one must wait as they would be a danger to themselves and others; they all agreed that on reaching the road, each party would press on back to the Magic Garden, whether they met up with the others or not. The plan was agreed.

Poppelana rose gracefully and, with a sense of urgency, gathered her family around her and quickly ensured that they all understood what was about to happen. She made them promise that they would leave with Monty when he gave the word.

Finally, she asked Massey - one of the taller of the chestnut ponies - to step forward.

'If I do not return, Massey, I ask you as the eldest of my children to lead in my place.' And she nudged his nose on each side with her own, sealing her choice.

Efa and his followers were ready. Effortlessly, they swung themselves up onto Poppelana's slender back from the log that they had previously sat on. Sitting in their customary four rows of three, they looked regal and ready for battle.

The rest of the Shepony herd now faced their leader and knelt before her. With a lump in her throat, she smiled and turned, and with a swish of white tail trotted out of the clearing and back towards Rowan Hill.

Exactly one hour later, Monty asked the other 85 ponies to get ready to leave.

The ponies rose and formed a line. Standing side by side in rows of five, Monty was touched by their serenity; but sensing their apprehension underneath, he reassured them. Seeing this calm, bold cat in front of them, the herd settled properly, and Monty made his way to the front.

With Poppelana and the stick people weighing heavily on his mind, Monty began to lead the Sheponies. Keeping a steady pace, he steered the herd of tiny animals toward the edge of the wood, on the first part of their journey back towards the Magic Garden

Chapter Seven

An Incredible Tunnel

Mr Leafblower's mind kept drifting back to Monty and the stick riders. He cared deeply about them, and wondered almost constantly what had happened to his friends.

Deep in his heart, however, he had a sense that they were safe! He had spent his whole life listening to his own heart on such matters, and was always right.

With this in mind, a feeling of joy spread right over Mr Leafblower, and having also made a delightful new friend (Pinbean), he began to whistle. He was a very good-humoured person, even at the worst of times.

Sooty wagged along with Mr Leafblower's whistled tune, and Pinbean swayed from side to side, riding on his 'poodle-horse.' The ground here was crisp and made walking easy, and there was a definite freshness in the air. All three seemed to have quite forgotten that danger could at any moment be close by.

Mr Leafblower, Sooty, and Pinbeam also of course had no idea that as they walked along so happily, 85 tiny Sheponies were making their way out of the wood, led by Monty. And they had no idea that on the higher ground of Rowan Hill, Poppelana - the leader of the Sheponies - was kicking furiously at rocks that would tumble dustily down and distract the evil Thworgs.

How amazed they would have been if they could have seen the clever fingers of their stick friends releasing lots of sore Shepony hooves from cruelly tied Thworg ropes! All of this was happening, not that far away, at the very time that Mr Leafblower felt the joy spreading through him and had begun to whistle!

'Oh, what a tremendous blue--' and only after at least three minutes of silence, which even for Mr Leafblower was a very long pause, did Sooty interrupt the rhythm of his happy walk and curve his head upwards to look at his friend. He was wondering why he had not heard him utter the last word of his sentence. Sooty had added the word '--sky' in his head. But why hadn't Mr Leafblower said it out loud?

Now he turned and saw what had stopped his leafy friend! For the second time that day, Sooty was faced with his old enemies, the Greenlings. But this time it was not one little Greenling he saw; he gulped as he took in the size of the problem!

A pyramid of Greenlings, standing at least two metres wide and a metre high, stood in front of the happy travellers and seemed to fill the whole field. They looked very cross. Mr Leafblower had spotted them first.

Then, in unison, the whole lot of the Greenlings

in the pyramid pointed and began to chant: 'We are the Greenlings and you have our brother!'

'Why have you kidnapped our brother?' they now chanted, louder, and stared menacingly at Mr Leafblower and Sooty.

Sooty let out a yelp and quivered with fear.

Mr Leafblower, however, without hesitation stepped towards the angry mob of Greenlings.

In a booming voice that rang out above their chorus of voices he announced: 'I am Mr Leafblower of the compost heap, resident tunnel-dweller of the Magic (long pause) Garden.

'And,' he continued, 'Rescuer of the small Greenling known as Pinbean.'

At once the pile of Greenlings rolled apart, and now they stood crowded together, hands on hips, hushed, and faced the three.

Pinbean hopped down from Sooty's back and ran to his family, who all began pat his little body with their small hands (a warm Greenling greeting.)

'You are found, you are found!' they said happily as they patted him.

Pinbean's smile at being reunited with his family stretched across his whole round body. He hastily recounted to them how Sooty and Mr Leafblower had helped him. Without them, he said, he would still be left crying alone in the field - and goodness knows what might have happened to him then! He told his family of the kindness that had been shown to him by his new friends, jumping for joy as he did because he was so happy to be in a family of Greenlings again.

Realising that in fact they owed a great debt of gratitude to another tunnel-dweller, and a curly-haired four-legged creature that they were sure they had met before, several Greenling elders stepped forward to proclaim their thanks to Sooty and Mr Leafblower.

A small wooden wheelbarrow was pushed towards them, stacked high with pale yellowy-green juicy gooseberries.

'Ah, a great Greenling delicacy, and my favourite!' was the last Sooty heard from Mr Leafblower for at least half an hour. He sat down right beside this juicy present and ate and ate and ate.

Tentatively, Sooty sniffed, and then licked, and then chewed, a gooseberry. As the juice squirted on his tongue, he decided he quite liked them and ate three more - but that was quite enough, for in truth he wasn't really sure if he liked them or not!

The Greenlings, however, liked the gooseberries very much so, and a little gooseberry party was now in full swing. Sooty sat and watched in amazement as the Greenlings between slurping gooseberries and entertaining him with several incredible acrobatic displays.

The Greenlings loved making different shapes by standing on top of each other: a giant triangle, then a square, and then a towering oblong. After each display, they would roll apart and form a perfect Greenling circle, and bow proudly towards Sooty and his eating friend.

'What fun!' Sooty thought, and he jumped and barked and ran around.

It was just as the Greenlings toppled apart once again, having formed a complicated hexagon with their bodies, that the sky above them suddenly darkened. A cold wind rasped down unexpectedly, hitting those below, and lingered.

Mr Leafblower leapt up and shouted, 'Take cover!' as he realised at once that it must be the dreaded Thworgs coming closer than they could have imagined.

And that's just what they did. To Sooty and Mr Leafblower's surprise, the Greenlings were disappearing into the ground fast, just by an old plum tree that they had not even noticed. Now they beckoned to Mr Leafblower and Sooty to join them.

'Quick! Come with us!' they shouted, 'Quick! Come!'

Not needing any more encouragement, Sooty and Mr Leafblower too headed down into the round hole that had a grassy doorway cut into the ground. It was expertly pulled closed as soon as they were inside, leaving the field above bare to searching eyes.

The blackness of the tunnel posed no problem for Greenlings, whose sight was much better underground.

Mr Leafblower could manage with a squint to see, but poor old Sooty saw only darkness.

A quick flick of a torch flooded light towards the little dog. Mr Leafblower seemed to have at least one of everything in his many pockets! Finding a torch had been no problem.

'We're safe now.' Mr Leafblower stroked his friend. From the light of the torch, the smooth solid sides of the tunnel were expertly illuminated. 'These Greenlings know how to tunnel!' he said to himself, and then, with a few pauses, he said it to Sooty.

There was no end in sight as the smooth tunnel snaked away into the distance, turning only to avoid tree roots.

'Well I never, well I--never!' exclaimed Mr Leafblower, 'Saved by Greenlings! Who would ever have--'

But Sooty heard no more; he was instead listening intently and sniffing the air. Yes, he thought, he did recognise that smell... but he could not at first place it.

Concentrating his very hardest, he thought and thought - and then it came to him! The scent was... could it be... yes! Now he was sure it was the scent of Sheponies - but how?

Chapter Eight

Tom Visits the Garden

Tom was thrilled to be coming to the Magic Garden on Sunday. It was his absolute favourite place. He had already shared many amazing adventures with the girls, including once being shrunk to a tiny size by lupin dust! He could hardly wait to see the animals and strange characters who lived in its many secret places.

Running up the drive happily past the spiky holly trees, Tom could never have guessed that many of those who lived there were involved in a dangerous rescue. But everything changed a few minutes later when he met his friends Holly and Victoria out on the neat green lawn.

Holly's voice was agitated and Tom could tell that his friend was worried about something.

'Oh, Tom we have so, so much to tell you!' she began.

First, Tom heard all about how the girls had met Ian, the Chinese green dragon. He was miffed that he had not been there to meet such an amazing visitor, and couldn't help thinking how much fun it would have been. Tom thought to himself that he too would have liked to have been given his own mooncake fortune cookie and tasted jasmine tea!

Victoria continued the story of their last few days in the magic garden while Holly caught her breath, explaining that there had been some unsettling news brought by the dragon. Tom listened, wide-eyed, as he heard about the miniature Sheponies. His amazement then turned immediately to horror as he heard about their capture by the evil Thworgs.

'Thworgs!' Tom almost shouted, he was so surprised to hear that the horrible creatures were involved. He had not heard mention of these dark beings for a long time but knew they always spelt trouble for the magic garden and all of its good inhabitants.

Next, the girls told him about the garden meeting called by Monty, and the decision to travel to the hill and offer help. The decision to help didn't surprise him, as he knew how kind those who lived in the magic garden were.

Twisting her white paper hanky around her fingers while she talked, Holly explained more, and eventually came to the end of her story. 'It was yesterday morning that we rode our bikes to the gate of the first field. We don't know what to do now, Tom. It really is awful just waiting and waiting, never knowing whether they are in trouble or if they need our help.'

Tom put his arms around his two friends. This was a scary time in the magic garden, and he needed a little time to digest all that he had just heard.

'Let's fetch Cinnamon and Treacle,' Victoria suggested eventually. 'I know that they are dying to see you, Tom, and they might have heard something during the night.'

The girls had promised the guinea pigs that they would lift them out of their pretty wooden hutch as soon as Tom arrived. Actually, Cinnamon and Treacle were quite capable of sliding the catch themselves, but they were such lazy lumps!

On their way to the guinea pig hutch, lots of birds and rabbits, and several of the frogs from the pond, stopped to greet the children and to ask for any news of Monty.

'None yet,' was the children's sad reply to the many little animals who were seeking reassurance. It was their reply, too, to Cinnamon and Treacle once they had taken them out of their hutch and further into the garden.

Making their way to the back of the garden, they reached the spot where the grass was left to grow quite long. Mum had insisted that some of the garden be left unkempt, providing a little haven for insects. Tiny moths flew through the meadow grass and leggy wildflowers grew here and there. Brightly spotted ladybirds darted about their business. This is where they sat, having found a patch of clover for Cinnamon and Treacle to munch away at.

The friends talked together and comforted each other, and were just about to head to the house to have some lunch when a flapping of wings above caught their attention.

Holly gasped. 'At last!'

Barbara the wood pigeon's familiar grey wings were directly above them, and she was about to land right in the middle of the little group. Breathless from her flight, she had returned as fast as she could to tell them what little she knew.

All of the garden's inhabitants quickly gathered to hear her news. Even the big chubby badger shuffled out, nearly colliding with three long-legged hares who had bounded over. Poor badger - he could hardly see where he was going in the daylight!

The blue-green dragonflies hovered, landing now and again on the carpet of grass. Tiny stick people had tumbled down from the tangled branches above and sat beside and on top of the others. Everyone needed to know whether Monty and the rest of their friends were safe

And just as Barbara opened her little beak to tell them everything, something else rather amazing happened.

From beneath the ground, an array of Blue Treeglies swept upwards like a giant firework, spinning patterns of light. Even in the daylight they shone bright blue, mesmerising everyone.

All those watching felt a tingling as they sensed the calmness these shiny good spirits of the garden brought. Seeing the look of wonder on Tom's face, Holly quickly explained to him about the treeglies, who he had never encountered before.

'These are the good spirits of the garden - a bit like fairies,' she said, smiling at her friend's stunned expression.

Tom was enjoying the display; though he did think that blue treeglies were fantastic, he also thought they looked nothing like he imagined fairies to be! Spinning and whirling, they too now settled amongst the animals, emitting friendly sapphire light.

Everyone had come, such was the importance of the events that had taken place recently in the magic garden. And all eyes were now glued to the wood pigeon who sat before them.

Sitting quiet and still now they listened, an atmosphere of tranquil calm emanating from the treeglies. Barbara told them what she knew, and it was worth the wait.

They learnt that their friends had safely contacted the poor hunted herd of Sheponies, and that soon, together with the leader of the herd, they intended to mount a rescue!

With a flurry of her wings, Barbara finished, 'If they are successful, soon they could be home in the magic garden!'

Now everyone saw clearly what must be done. Preparations must be made in readiness, for the garden may soon need to house a herd of homeless little ponies who had suffered a terrible ordeal. A fine welcome for their own brave friends would need to be put on. Volunteers began at once to take on tasks for the homecoming!

The stick people would decorate the branches of the trees, helped by the dragon-flies: fine silver thread would link the branches and would be decorated with the pretty honeysuckle berries. Delicate white jasmine flowers would be strung between.

The rabbits and hares would bake chunky apple pies and delicate plum puddings, using only the best fruit of the garden. The badgers would play music and must polish their instruments and rehearse. Discarded bits of wood and logs could be linked together to form tables for the feast!

The honey bees, too, would join in, and lace the dishes with their delectable lavender honey. The children's task would be to explore the seven acres of garden and decide upon the best place to hide a herd of extremely small ponies! And they must make it ready with hay as the Sheponies would be hungry, and buckets of water for them to drink.

No one said the unthinkable: that the rescue might fail, and that their friends might not make it back. They knew instinctively that to dwell on failure would be to let their friends down.

'We are where we are,' Badger said, philosophically, in his deep baritone voice. He then moved off quickly to find the rest of his band.

And so the garden was alive with activity. Animals went scuttling this way and that with a great sense of purpose, excited and sure of the prospect of Monty's success.

Not all in the garden had joined in, however. Amongst all of the hustle and bustle, the blue treeglies disappeared; while everyone else hurried around them, they quietly slipped away to the back of the garden. They then glided, unnoticed, to the compost heap, the entrance to Mr Leafblower's den.

Still unseen by all except by a little ant carrying a small frayed brown leaf, the blue treeglies then glided under the locked door of Mr Leafblower's home. Once inside, they followed the metal ladder and, shining brightly, they lit up his den like a hundred blue light bulbs.

The treeglies were just passing through, though; for they headed out from his back door into the dark tunnel that housed his Leaf Flume. Then, as suddenly as they had arrived, they were gone, spinning and looping down the very tunnel that the children had once travelled while riding on Mr Leafblower's flume (the same tunnel that, not so long ago, Sooty had been trapped in by the angry Greenlings.)

The treeglies flew on down the tunnel, and on, and on, and on. Who could say exactly where they go?

Chapter Nine

Under Attack

Poppelana pressed her slender back into the hillside, able to rest at last; her whole body shuddered as she gulped in air. Her journey to the east side of the hill had been treacherous, yet she had survived, and only once had nearly been detected by drifting Thworgs.

She searched now with her eyes for a rocky patch where she would be able to cause the small avalanche that must distract the enemy. Aware that the stick riders would be waiting, she lost no time. Creeping forward and down, she dug her hoof into the hillside and began her task.

Efa, chief of the stick people, heard the clatter of falling rocks and signalled his party.

Small enough to seek shelter amongst the thick long grass, the stick warriors began to move. They had had the shackled Sheponies in their sight for a while.

The captured ponies stood huddled together, fearful and folorn, with their little hooves tied. They had begun to give up hope; Efa could read it in their drawn faces.

The hope was that most of the enemy would now go to the east side of the hill to investigate the avalanche that Poppelana had caused. And that is exactly what they did, full of wrath for anyone who would dare to disturb their hill, Thworg Hill!

Each hoof of the little Sheponies had firstly been snared by Thworg rope, and then joined by the hooves to the rest of the ponies by webs of thick twine. Efa had counted fourteen ponies tied in this way; with the time he had lying low in the grass, he managed to allocate a pony to each of his brave team. He himself would free three, no blade could match Efa's.

Every one of the stick people carried a dagger of blackened oak, thinner and sharper than any razor blade a human could have owned, tucked inside their red foxglove boots. First they would whisper their presence to every pony, who must try to remain calm while they took up position. On Efa's signal, the cutting would begin, and only when all fourteen ponies' feet were free would they dare to climb aboard their backs ready to leave.

After working in complete silence, the ponies would then be ridden down the hill by their friends, the stick people. The stick riders would reassure the scared creatures and carefully direct them down. If the enemy Thworgs attacked again, the riders would protect them, fighting their persecutors without yielding, and using their almost invisible size to their advantage.

The stick people knew that despite their and the Sheponies' exhaustion, they must insist that the ponies move quickly once they were freed. They must find the strength to trot, then canter, then gallop, because as soon as the silence was broken by their movement, the Thworgs would be alerted.

Back at the edge of the wood, Monty too was busy. Having surveyed the open ground at the edge of the wood and told the herd of Sheponies he was in charge of to get ready, he waited.

Monty's heart was beating rapidly and his muscles were taut as he thought about the journey ahead. As soon as the dust and rocks could be detected from Poppelana's avalanche, they would leave. Swiftly and without stopping, the Sheponies would run and run, following their cat friend down and along the well-trodden paths in the woods that they knew by heart, and then on across the fields. On and on they would run, until they reached the gate, and then the road where Monty gambled Thworgs would not dare to cross for fear of human detection. But he could not be sure: they had grown in arrogance and daring. For who could have guessed that Thworgs would take the Sheponies' home in the first place?

If spirit and goodness would win the day, he knew he had it in the wonderful creatures he now led. They were willing to put complete faith in this leader of the magic garden, and he in turn had faith in them.

Then, all of a sudden, it began.

Taken by surprise, Monty saw the grotesque bleak forms of the Thworgs rising and heading towards the east side of the hill. Monty saw what seemed like smoke, but immediately knew it to be the dust of the rocks! Up on the hill itself, Efa saw it too, and signalled to his army.

The herd of Sheponies with Monty at the lead now tore away from their wooded refuge and sped out into the open. Careering down, the ponies ran faster than they had ever ran. Running for their lives, they kept close together, occasionally bumping and jostling one another. Their tiny legs seemed to lift from the ground completely, such was their pace, and on they went. Their effort was immense and Monty felt proud of them.

A few Thworgs had remained to guard those Sheponies bound by ropes at the top of the hill, but now they swooped and shrieked in anger as they saw beneath them the larger herd that they had never managed to capture galloping away. The thought that the main herd had successfully hidden from them in such close proximity clawed into them, increasing their anger, and they gave chase, piercing the air with their horrible sound.

Seizing this moment, Efa and the stick people began to slice through the ropes holding the fourteen prisoners at the top of Rowan hill, now foolishly left unguarded by the Thworgs.

The captive Sheponies held still as their slender legs were freed and did not even dare whinny. It was now their turn to escape. The stick riders now crept up onto their backs, and the little group turned together, obeying the precise timing of their riders' pressed heels which guided their movements.

Quietly, they formed a line and then, at Efa's silent signal, they were off, ridden away by tiny stick people. As they flew down the hill after Monty and the rest of their friends, they began to see and hear the commotion below. Far away in the patchwork of fields, they could just make out the main herd with Monty at the head. The next thing they saw, with shock, was the enormous black cloud of Thworgs advancing upon their friends. There wasn't time to watch - nor could they bear to. Hastily they continued to plough down the jagged paths that they hoped would eventually lead to freedom.

Efa was aware that they could do no other than virtually follow the same route as Monty and the others if they were to make it home. His small group were for now behind the enemy, and as luck would have it undetected.

However, they needed to make use of any shelter they could. They had been lucky so far, able to ride through open space because of Poppelana's distraction.

Now, riding at the front, Efa could see the beginnings of small trees and bushes forming a natural boundary to hide them from the Thworgs, and he steered the little chestnut pony he was riding towards it.

'The hedgerow will give a little cover, press in close!' Efa passed the word back as he led his party.

The eerie piercing shrieks of Thworgs now filled the air and terrified them all. The stick riders felt the shuddering of the ponies, but they forced them on. Soon they would reach the wood and follow the exact path Monty had taken.

Monty had reached the first field before he heard the noise and felt the first chill of Thworgs descending. A great deal of ground had been covered by this time; the Sheponies with him could hardly continue at this pace for much longer. As they galloped, they sometimes collided. They kept running, though, knowing that escape was more important than their aching limbs.

Monty was no ordinary cat, and his feline legs carried him faster than any pony. At the entrance to the second field, he tore across the opening, shouting behind him to the ponies following, urging them on.

'This way! We're nearly there!'

They continued to follow, but for some it was proving too much and the herd had begun to split.

Several of the younger ponies could not keep up.
Feeling again the ominous cold penetrating his fur,
Monty looked back up.

Only a hundred feet above them and already halfway
across the first field, a vast cloud of black Thworg bodies
was in pursuit - and now he saw that they were moving
faster than the ponies!

The Thworgs were gaining ground and Monty knew
it. He also knew that the gate was still a long way off, as
the last of his charge thundered through into the second
field. Running at great speed, he turned his head again

and with shock saw a black shape appear almost directly in front of him. It seemed to appear from nowhere, and now stood facing him only a few feet away. Monty's heart skipped a beat.

Chapter Ten

Sooty Saves the Day

Mr Leafblower was still musing over the fact that he and Sooty had been helped by Greenlings, who were known far more for their grumpiness than their helpfulness! He was also angry, because once again he thought about the enemy who had caused such unhappiness and despair among the animals, even if new friendships had been forged.

'How dare these dreadful Thworgs hunt other animals in this way!'

Now he sat down with the Greenling elders, and first thanked them for saving Sooty and himself by letting them come through their grass door from the field above. Next, he told them the reason he and his friend had been in the field. The Greenlings had saved their lives and therefore they deserved to be told everything; Greenlings might be grumpy, but they were fair.

By the time Mr Leafblower had finished the story of the Sheponies and their rescuers adventures, the Greenlings had begun to chant. 'Evil Thworgs, give back the land!'

Leaning backwards, having completed his story, Mr Leafblower couldn't help once again to notice the tunnel sides. Comparing this excellent workmanship to his own, he was very impressed. He could talk tunnel-making for many hours because it was his favourite topic!

Dragging him back out of these tunnel thoughts, though, was the rather annoying continuous pulling of his leafy sleeve by his four-legged companion. Sooty had been desperately trying to get his attention.

'I can smell them, I can smell them!' Sooty panted, and began to wag his tail. 'Sheponies, Sheponies!' And Sooty began to bark with excitement.

Mr Leafblower's eyes widened with astonishment. The Greenling elders were intrigued that the little dog could smell anything in their tunnel, which up until then they considered entirely smell-proof!

'Well, well, well!' said one of the Greenlings and quickly all of the others, who were given to repetition, joined in with a chorus of: 'Well, well, well! Well, well, well!'

Suddenly, an even bigger noise could be heard like the banging of a million drums above them - and it seemed to be getting louder with every beat.

Within seconds, a kind of periscope was pushed up through a cup-size flap in the tunnel door above them by the Greenlings. One of the Greenling elders looked out to see what on earth could be causing the racket.

The noise got louder, and now the Greenling, with a look of dismay, first beckoned to Mr Leafblower and then to Sooty.

What they saw through his periscope made their hearts jump. Dashing through the field and running for dear life was Monty - and right behind him were what looked like hundreds of tiny horses. Some were black, some chestnut, some white! They were gorgeous, and just as Sooty had imagined them to be, except even smaller!

But now Sooty yelped as he saw what they were running from: a bleak, heavy darkness above, which he knew could only be one thing. It was the Thworgs, and they were nearly on top of them!

'Quick, we must save them!' Mr Leafblower boomed.

The Greenling elders made haste. This was the perfect opportunity to repay the kindness shown to their own Pinbean and, even more than this, a perfect time to teach those evil Thworgs a lesson.

The grass door into the field was swung open. Now, quickly and without hesitation, Sooty scrambled back out into the field. He began to run towards the stampede of horses, barking loudly so that Monty would see him. He must show them all the way into the tunnel before it was too late!

Meanwhile, Greenlings dragged planks of wood that had been stored neatly along the sides of their tunnel. A long walkway was being formed, which would make it easier for the retreating animals to run down. There was little time, but Greenlings were very fast and organised.

They ran all around the tunnel like marbles, spreading out, grabbing the planks and tools and nails. The wooden planks seemed to skim along the ground by themselves. In fact, they were being rolled into place by groups of helpful Greenlings who had pulled their legs into their bodies so that they could roll. Working at tremendous speed, they fixed them neatly in place. All of this had taken only seconds to do.

When Monty had seen a black figure appear in front of him, he feared the worst and had yelled at the pack behind him to stop. Now he recognised the black curly coat and made out the shape of his dog friend: not a Thworg after all! He had never been so glad to see Sooty in his life.

'Follow me, follow me!' Sooty did not wait for an answer, and after all, there wasn't time.

Spinning round, he turned back towards the Greenling door as soon as he saw that Monty had recognised him. Monty swiftly followed. Glancing to his side, he now passed Mr Leafblower, who stood not far from the door. There was only time to exchange a mutual glance of relief. His leafy friend would wait and ensure the last of the ponies got through; there would be time to speak later.

The exhausted Sheponies followed their cat leader and tumbled through the Greenling door, down the wooden plank, and into the blackness of the tunnel. The loud clatter of tiny hooves reverberated through the tunnel walls. Hundred of hooves thumped the ground above as they ran to reach the door; and to the small round Greenlings lining the tunnel, it sounded like rocks raining onto the ground above them. They covered their little ears with their hands.

The last of the ponies travelled down the plank, crashing into those in front and squeezing them through. But it didn't matter - once inside they were safe!

Then Mr Leafblower grabbed the door to pull it closed. Aghast, he saw back in the field a small white pony that had fallen. It must have been one of the last.

Now he could see it clearly, lying on its back and trying desperately to right itself. Its tiny Shepony legs waved furiously in the air, but it just did not have the strength to turn itself back onto its feet.

Then the legs stopped and it lay motionless. It would be left to the mercy of the evil throng that was nearly upon it; this small creature would take the brunt of their anger. Mr Leafblower's heart nearly burst with sorrow. And now, without a thought for his own safety, he ran towards the pony as though shot from a catapult.

Seeing him dash away at the last minute, the Greenling leader shouted after him: 'Come back, come back, dear friend, there is no time!'

Breathlessly, ignoring the Greenlings' calls, Mr Leafblower reached the young pony and, bending down, scooped it into his sturdy arms. The air around him had chilled, and a horrible feeling crept through his body.

The Thworgs were visible now. He could even make out their hollow eyes, searching for prey. The little warm body that he held trembled.

But Mr Leafblower's heart was strong and kind, and it protected him for a moment. This moment was all he needed; his very goodness of character sheltered him from the Thworgs' cold and heartless view as he flew back towards the door, throwing himself and his bundle through it. It was pulled closed immediately behind him.

Not a sound was made now in the tunnel. The enemy was directly above. The ground they moved across froze temporarily as they passed over it, thawing only when they had gone. The residents of the tunnel remained hushed and huddled together in the darkness.

A message from Monty was passed down the line of ponies: 'You are safe; do not be afraid of the dark; remain quiet and still. We are guests of the Greenlings and this is their tunnel.'

The Greenlings, too, tried to reassure the little ponies by patting them gently, a traditional Greenling gesture of welcome. However, Monty could still sense the wariness and remaining fear felt among the herd.

Suddenly Monty was aware that the Greenlings had begun to stare back down their own tunnel, where it snaked away into the distance. The Greenlings knew every sight and sound associated with their tunnel, and they were now alerted to the fact that something was approaching.

Seconds later, Monty could sense it too. Something or someone was travelling towards them all - not from above, but from far away, deep within the recesses of the tunnel.

Now there was a rustling of activity as the small green creatures marched down the tunnel, wondering who dared to enter without invitation. How bravely they marched on, intent on protecting their guests!

It soon became evident that none of them need have worried. Together, all in the tunnel saw the light appear: fast and floating, it shone luminous and bright. As it travelled further forwards, the whole tunnel took on a blue haze which revealed every nook and crevice of the walls and floor. A warmth crept through those huddled, accompanied by a feeling of peace and calm.

The blue treeglies glided and hovered like a thousand lights above their friends. The light they created allowed the little ponies to blink and see their surroundings, as well as their strange hosts.

Monty stood, tail high, greeting his blue friends. The treeglies had come to guide them back home through the mass of tunnels; how thrilled they were to see them! And how the blue treeglies now were needed, because one wrong turn could take the party many miles in the wrong direction. Still many of the tunnels remained unexplored, housing new friends or even those who are best left undisturbed. Some of the tunnels belonged to others unknown even to the Greenlings, and for now those who lived in the magic garden had enough to deal with!

As soon as he had greeted the treeglies, Monty sensed the intense exhaustion of the Sheponies and passed the order to rest down the line. Tiredness took over quickly, and fifteen minutes later, the warm breath of sleeping ponies could be seen in the blue glow of the Greenling tunnel.

Sooty and Mr Leafblower almost leapt upon Monty, such was their joy at seeing him. They talked in whispers so as not to wake the sleeping ponies, each taking a turn to tell all that they had seen and done during the past three days since leaving their garden home. The Greenling elders joined them, bringing warm sweet gooseberry drinks for which they were very grateful.

Refreshed and rested, Monty took on a serious air. Glad to be in the safety of the tunnel, he knew however that he could not remain here. Dear friends were still in terrible danger, and they must be his priority now. The blue treeglies would guide the herd through the snaking tunnels safely back to the magic garden. But what about the others? Had Efa and his stick warriors managed to descend the hill safely? They must be found!

Monty saw Popellana clearly in his mind's eye, hardly daring to think about what may have befallen her after putting herself at such risk. How sad he felt, knowing that her chances against hordes of Thworgs - now angry and seeking revenge - were slim indeed.

This image of his friend now sparked Monty to action. With renewed energy, he addressed the Greenlings with an unexpected request.

Chapter Eleven

Monty Goes Back

All at once, the tunnel was alive with the clopping of hooves as the ponies got to their feet. Rested and no longer afraid, they formed a line. They were happy to be guided to the magic garden via this underground labyrinth, nuzzling each other and smiling as they clomped along. As they travelled, the Blue Treeglies hovered high in single file above them, snug to the tunnel roof: a moving lantern shining the way and keeping in perfect time with the steady trotting procession. This was a procession led by a very proud black dog, too, who had been braver than he could have ever imagined he could be!

It had been decided that the main herd would go back to the garden at once. Monty had no intention of returning with them; he would find the others. His unusual request for help from his new Greenling friends was greeted with an enthusiastic 'yes.'

The Greenling periscope was pushed upwards through the grass, revealing the land above. There was no sign of the Thworgs. The field seemed deceptively peaceful, given what had happened earlier in the day. No one spoke.

Monty and Mr Leafblower were the first to emerge into the field. The sun was no longer bright, and dusk was now mere minutes away; the smell of damp grass filled the air, as a little rain had recently fallen. About fifty Greenlings too hopped out of the doorway and into the field above. Once there, they stood straight and tidy awaiting Monty's orders.

The Greenlings, camouflaged by their round grass-like bodies, blended into the field perfectly. They had needed no persuasion to join Monty in his search for Efa and the remaining fourteen ponies. Truthfully they preferred being underground, wrapped in the safety of their tunnel walls, but they were brave and wanted to help. So determined were they to be helpful that they made a special effort to hide their nervousness.

Thoughts swirled inside Monty's head: If Efa had managed to escape he must be headed this way, following the very same route: the only sure way home. One cat alone would be unable to spot them quickly. But if that cat was high enough, his bright eyes could see for miles - especially with the binoculars Mr Leafblower had dug out of one of his many pockets!

Poppelana's fate was also on his mind.

Jolting back out of these thoughts, by the breath of a cool northern wind against his whiskers, he now addressed his little gang of green helpers.

'Form the tower!' he directed his friends.

At once, the Greenlings began to roll into action, stacking themselves ten at the bottom, then nine on top of then, then eight and so on until finally there were just two at the very top.

'Ready?' Monty shouted - and, without waiting for an answer, he deftly climbed this Greenling tower and balanced himself gently on top.

Steadying himself on two legs, Monty scanned the surrounding area, but he could see no sign of his friends, and thankfully none of the enemy. He sought again, squinting his eyes and concentrating hard, but still he saw nothing.

'They must be out there.' He spoke out loud but expected no reply and, again moving his head left and right, looked for any clue of a cluster of tiny ponies. Not one to give up easily, he scanned the surrounding landscape once more, sweeping the fields desperately with his shining green eyes.

Then he saw it. Something white was moving somewhere down there: his eyes were drawn towards a section of brambles that skirted along the field just beyond this one. Once again, he trained the binoculars there. Had something moved? – his whiskers switched with anticipation, he looked again, closer this time beneath a clump of small bushes. His heart leapt. Stretching the very muscles of his eyes, he could just make out a small group moving slowly down.

It was Efa and the ponies, he was sure! And they were safe!

He shouted the news to his Greenling friends and scrambled down his unusual look-out post. They now toppled to the ground and as soon as his paws touched the grass they threw their tiny arms up in the air to celebrate. Mr Leafblower jumped high on the spot with joy, and then he carefully tucked away his precious binoculars into a deep leaf pocket.

'I will bring them back to the door - be ready!' said Monty, as he bounded away back up the hillside, towards the place he now knew they were.

'Be careful, be careful!' he heard them all chant as he ran, but he wasn't thinking of his own safety. Fear for the safety of his Shepony friends gave him extra speed. The enemy Thworgs were close and the blackness could return at any moment.

Skimming the hedges of hawthorn and blackthorn, he sped on.

Meanwhile, Efa heard a sound and signalled to his band of riders and ponies to stop. He listened intently. It was the rustling of an approach, he was now sure, and he unsheathed his lethal black oak blade.

Monty, knowing he was close to where he had spotted his lost friends, shouted out - and could only hope that he had been heard! He was very aware that a stick warrior could administer a severe wound.

Seconds later, they collided - but not in battle, thankfully! Spotting each other all of a sudden, Efa and Monty embraced with happiness. The plan had worked!

The little ponies had jostled, scared at the intrusion, but were quickly reassured by their riders. Here was Monty, cat-guardian of the magic garden, they whispered into the ears of the Sheponies in their gentle sing-song voices.

Monty smiled as he cast his eye across these wonderful creatures ridden so well by great horsemen and women, riders who normally occupied the branches of the tall fir trees in the magic garden. They were quite tiny seated high on the backs of these horses, even though the ponies themselves were very small!

'Any lost or hurt?' he enquired of his friend.

'None, sir,' replied Efa.

'Come, Efa, you have done well. Quickly - there is no time to waste - we have been extremely fortunate to have found an unexpected way home.'

Leading the last of the herd back towards the soft mossy door, Monty briefly explained to Efa, his riders, and the Sheponies that it was the so-called 'angry' Greenlings of the eastern tunnel who had helped to save them all!!

The stick riders thought this very odd because of the Greenlings' unusually unhelpful reputations! The details would be repeated over many days, perhaps even many years, back in the warmth and security of the magic garden. However, now they must concentrate on getting the Sheponies safely underground.

The tired group of travellers could see something sticking upwards in the field as they approached. Two Greenling elders held open the door that led deep down into the earth below, and Mr Leafblower smiled kindly as he counted the ponies and their riders in. The little horses were nervous as they passed these creatures, that looked a bit like giant apples with legs! They had never seen anyone quite like that before - but they now trusted their companions completely, and hurried past.

At last they could rest for the first time in a long while. And that's just what they did! These last ponies lay down on the tunnel floor, and as they did so, they too were gently patted by the little Greenlings. The sores that bore witness to their cruelly tied hooves were bathed, soothing ointment applied, and bandaged where necessary.

The eastern tunnel was busy once again: tiny ponies walked down its corridors, intermingling with hundreds of Greenlings who now and then formed a pile and slept. Greenlings were, after all, still creatures of habit!

The stick riders drank heartily the gooseberry juice and munched on the cherry biscuits they were given, and then, after checking that each pony was settled for the night, they too slept soundly.

An hour later, Monty sent word down the tunnel to Efa and Mr Leafblower to meet with him back at the grass door. They had already guessed that Monty meant once again to leave the safety of the tunnel. All three needed no reminder that one of their party was still in grave danger.

Monty was resolute: it was pointless risking anymore lives. Mr Leafblower would take these ponies, and reunite them as a full herd. His tunnel knowledge was second to none, and he would easily catch up with Sooty and the 85 little horses that had left several hours earlier. Their journey would be lit by the goodness of the light provided by the remaining Blue Treeglies. Monty would go on alone.

Mr Leafblower, head bowed, pushed open the grass door for his friend, wishing him the very best of luck. Efa had stripped himself of his most valuable possession - his dagger of blackened oak. It hung now, held by ivy twine, around Monty's neck.

None of the three spoke: they had no need for words. Instead, they looked into the bright pool of each others' eyes, where each saw hope.

As his charges woke, Efa explained to them that they would soon be with their friends, and to make preparations for the final part of their journey.

At this happy news, the ponies began to talk amongst themselves excitedly. They had heard stories about the magic garden - but never thought that they would actually live there!

Inevitably, some began to ask questions about the head of their herd. Where was Poppelana, when would she join them? they asked innocently, for they had not realised that Poppelana had not been seen by anyone since her journey to the far side of the hill.

Efa chose to ignore these questions for now. He did not want to upset the herd, and could only hope that no news was good news.

Chapter Twelve

Darkness Descends

Poppelana could do no more. Her hooves were scraped and her slender legs bled, such had been her furious efforts to dislodge as many rocks as she could. However, she felt no discomfort; instead she was elated. The avalanche of dust and stone tumbling down would surely be enough to make the Thworgs curious. In her mind's eye she saw again the grotesque forms of her enemy. They had stolen her land and hurt her people. She would not let them make slaves of the fourteen horses they had captured.

The coldness preceded them only by minutes. Poppelana knew they were close by. She also knew that there was nowhere to hide on this barren side of the hill.

A black shadow crept over the ground, blotting out the sunlight where it passed. She remained calm and her thoughts were with her herd. The longer she could keep them here, the greater chance the others would have of escape.

The coldness became sharper. An icy wind blew close, freezing the leaves on a small rowan tree that grew only meters from where she stood. Her black and white coat dampened as the air grew moist and they approached. There were no other living creatures, not even a bird, as all of the wild animals had fled when sensing the danger. Only Poppelana's frail shivering, tiny form stood against the cold wind.

It was time to move - to play for time, for the others.

Her thinking, though, had become confused, as a slicing pain squeezed through her head, caused by the plummeting temperature. Pushing herself, she began: one leg, then the next, - and at first stumbled. Bending her head forward, she painfully began to run.

By now, Poppelana was engulfed in a black, freezing thick cloud. She could see nothing ahead, but picked up speed, running blind. The direction did not matter, but she knew by the way her hooves felt the ground beneath them that she was moving downhill.

A terrible shrieking became part of the cloud that surrounded her. Her good heart struggled to keep at bay the horrible grasping of evil that wanted to possess her mind and soul. The swirling inside her head became too much, and she felt herself buckle. Her tiny head thumped the ground, and then she rolled, unable to keep to her feet. No longer could she withstand the malice of the dreadful Thworgs.

Something talon-like now grasped and grabbed at her body. It held her tightly, and she felt herself lifted higher and higher.

Is this death? she thought vaguely, before finally drifting into what seemed like a deep, deep sleep. Then her body became limp.

It was as though time had been suspended.

A gentle whispering seemed to penetrate her mind eventually, and she was aware of the absence of the terrible chill that before had paralysed her very soul. A warm glow touched her inside instead. Dare she open her eyes? she wondered.

Blinking her long black lashes open, she could see the blueness of the sky. Directly above her, the slow motion of an enormous green wing, beating slowly up and down, caused her to gasp.

Slowly gaining the rest of her senses again, she felt and saw the green, claw-like foot that managed to hold her tight without hurting her at all.

A world of fields appeared and passed below. Trying to make sense of what was happening, she remembered her fall.

Little puffs of white cloud splashed the blue sky around her, confirming what she thought – she was amongst the heavens – floating in the bluest of skies - then she knew for definite that she was being carried by some enormous creature. This creature was flying along, clutching her, and carrying her away - but where?

Something moved above: the foot that held her. The leg of the creature was thick and sturdy, and it too was emerald green like its wings. Now both shimmered in the sunlight.

A rope ladder had been dropped down the side of its leg. Poppelana could hardly believe it, but it was true: someone or something was making its way down the rope ladder towards her. Strangely, she found herself unafraid. Once again, she felt a surge of the tingly warmth that had woken her, and it seemed to fill her inside as well as out.

Slightly lifting her head, she watched - and now made out the shape of a four-legged animal. Her heart began to race as she recognised him. She wanted to call out to him to be careful but could find no words. Deftly, he descended the ladder, and ended up sitting right beside her.

Her friend now bent his head and carefully licked away the dirt that covered her grazed nose. Poppelana stretched her neck upward and again tried to talk, but she was too exhausted to utter a sound.

Monty spoke reassuringly to her. 'The Chinese green dragon is taking you home to the magic garden, Poppelana.'

His face alight with the pleasure of seeing her, he added, 'You have been asleep for quite a while.'

Monty stayed close to his friend. As they flew on, the sky began to darken as night time fell, and a million thoughts raced through her head.

Could it be true - had she been rescued? Where were her children, her herd? Had they been saved?

The darkness of the Thworgs crept into her mind, too, and all of the heartache they had caused.

Monty interrupted these thoughts, and whispered quietly into her soft ear. He told her all that had occurred as they travelled together through the night sky. Her bravery had given the others the few minutes they needed; the plan had worked! The news of her family safe was enough, and a new sense of happiness now poured into her, erasing for the time being her ordeal.

Night time brought the sounds of owls and the calling of foxes in the distance, and she wondered how long they had been airborne. Poppelana felt the change in the wind as the dragon began to drop, and knew they must be about to land.

Below, she saw the glint of soft moss and grass highlighted by an especially bright moon. Two meandering streams, winding paths, and trees alight with tiny lanterns were now clearly in view.

They circled and then floated down: a green misty vision to the animals and children waiting below.

Chapter Thirteen

The Homecoming

Lots was happening in the magic garden as Ian the dragon flew towards it, carrying his special passengers.

It was past midnight when the inhabitants of the garden heard unusual noises coming from the compost heap and began gathering near to it. In fact, the heap itself was moving as if it was coming alive!

Minutes later, Mr Leafblower himself erupted out of it, followed by a magnificent herd of Sheponies! Those standing close by were the first to set eyes on the teeny horses, and clapped and jumped with relief and happiness. The daring rescue had been successful!

Hearing the commotion, the news spread quickly as friends in the garden ran to tell each other. At once, the tall fir trees began to glow as stick people emerged from between the leaves and branches; quickly, they lit the hundreds of tiny conker lanterns that swung there.

The light from these and the moon revealed how busy everyone in the garden had been. The log tables were set out. Dashing hares and rabbits now placed on them the fine things to eat and drink; they had been meticulously prepared during the past few days.

Mr Badger's band, rehearsed and ready, struck up a familiar melody. And in the background the tuneful singing of the tiny stick people softly filled the evening air. Everyone felt restored, and the garden looked exquisite.

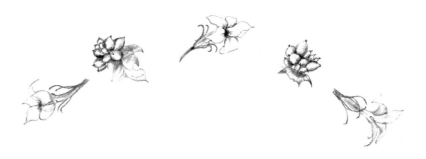

With such a feeling of joy, a little hum of voices began to sing their favourite song:

I went out to the Hazelwood
Because a fire was in my head
And cut and peeled a hazel wand
And hooked a berry to a thread

Meanwhile, Claudia and Barry the squirrels had scrambled through Monty's cat flap, and woken Holly and Victoria and Tom from the spare bedroom. The children had left strict instructions that they must be told immediately of any developments.

Thrilled by the news that the tiny horses had arrived in the garden the girls and Tom dashed outside. Spellbound, they watched and listened to all that was unfolding in the garden. Incredible though it all was, something even better happened next: the familiar sight of a little black poodle came trotting towards them.

'Sooty, Sooty!' shouted Vikki, as she hugged his neck.

Sooty leapt at his friends and licked them all! The children patted and cuddled him again and again – he was pleased, and could not resist two or three loud barks!

"Everything that has happened was written in your fortune cookie or should I say mooncake you know" said Holly stroking her friend.

Sooty looked unsure and so he carefully pulled the little piece of paper from the inside of his red collar where he kept any interesting bits and pieces.

"Read it out loud" said Tom wanting to know if it could really have foretold everything that had happened.

And once again in his clearest voice the little black poodle read the fortune he had been given in what seemed like a long time ago.

'Not north, not south, nor east but west
You will lead and guide the rest
They with little strength remaining
Run from ever blackness gaining
In the darkness light will pour
An enemy will share a door
what will be was always meant
The good will rise the bad are spent'

"Oh it was true" Tom gasped and as he began to fathom the poem outloud.

"**You** did travel west **and you did find the scent** of the little horses".

Now the girls joined in.

"The ponies were near exhaustion when you showed Monty the way to the tunnel" Holly added excitedly.

Sooty's tail began to wag faster and faster as each person spoke. He was such an happy little dog!

Vikki quickly answered the next line

"The angry Greenlings let us **use the door** into their tunnel and the tunnel was **lit by the blue treeglies**"

Sooty's tail was wagging so furiously now that he nearly fell over. He did however manage to have the last word, even though he was quite breathless. His little voice rang out into the night

"the Evil Thworgs are defeated hooray"

And now he added with a little jump " they are definitely **spent**."

At which point he tumbled head over tail making them all burst out laughing.

Back at the compost heap, Efa led the final group of Sheponies out of Mr Leafblower's den, immediately followed by hundreds of Greenlings who spilled out into the magic garden. The story of their helpfulness had already been shared, and they were made very welcome. In fact, it was on this very day that the

Greenlings became firm friends of the garden people and were never referred to as the **angry** Greenlings again. Instead, they now became forever known as **the good Greenlings of the Eastern Tunnel!**

The children were thrilled to see their friends again, and asked lots of questions - but where was Monty?

Mr Leafblower was ready with the answer.

'My dear - children,' he said brightly, 'Monty will-' and then, following the longest pause that Mr Leafblower had ever made, he finished his sentence with a fast '-arrive very very soon.'

A snowy white swan had brought the good news an hour before to Mr Leafblower and he was very excited and terribly relieved. Only Mr Leafblower had been told of Monty's intention to contact Madame Mole, and even he was not told why. For everyone's protection, they must only be told about a tiny piece of this part of Monty's plan, he had told his leafy friend.

* * * *

As soon as Monty had climbed the Greenling Tower the day before, he had spotted the fine bluish-brown wings of Madame Mole's moth. This meant that his friend Madame Mole had received his note.

'Thank goodness!' he had thought.

The last time Monty had seen his dear friend Madame Mole was when the children had needed help to rescue Sooty in the Greenling tunnel. How strange, he had thought, to be standing on top of these very Greenlings now.

Vague though he had had to be, Madame Mole had responded - and the help he so badly needed was here! His heart sang. Monty spoke the code that only two in the world knew, and could only hope that it would reach the banks of the Yangtze. Only word of mouth would do: there could be no written evidence. It would be told to Ian the Dragon, and only he would understand its full meaning:

'LAHM77W2117JA'

Monty whispered his coded message, and it was duly memorised by the small moth that had landed momentarily on his back: a creature that no one else had noticed at all, and that now flew quietly away.

Training his binoculars on the countryside around, he now began in earnest the task of searching for Efa and the lost ponies.

Chapter Fourteen

The Amazing Moonbeam

If the message got to the dragon, he would rendezvous with Monty at the side of the wood that lay half-way up Rowan Hill. If not, Monty must consider carefully the fate of those who he was the guardian of. Alone, he was more likely to fail. This could mean the loss of the Moonpiece - and if the Thworgs finally possessed the Moonpiece, they would wreak havoc on all of the creatures in and close to his magic garden. A shiver passed through him.

The only way Poppelana could be rescued now would be by the united power of two fragments of moon: one from each magic garden.

The Moonpiece that Monty had brought with him swayed as he moved his head from side to side. It was held in the tiny green velvet bag hung around his neck within a small wooden box. The box was no bigger than a small bird's egg. Next to it hung the dagger that Efa had loaned him.

It was a dangerous thing to remove the Moonpieces from their garden homes. If they were gone for long, the beautiful places that had grown from their magic energy would wither and die.

On this occasion alone he had chosen to take this chance. After all, he could go back if his friend did not arrive. Alone, he would not jepordise his people – the risk would be too great. The lives of **many** would have to be put before **one.**

Only the goodness of the Moonpieces could penetrate the vile black haze of Thworgs surrounding their friend. It could provide the way in – like a chink in a curtain. The element of surprise would help. The cat and the dragon together would cut through the cloud of the evil Thworgs like a knife through butter. Time would be accelerated. The two would ride on the moonbeam they had created by fusing together the two moon fragments.

It would shine just like a torch. And together they would ride its light!

Monty waited. The sky remained empty as he carefully searched it; doubt crept into his mind. A small moth could easily have been intercepted, even with the powerful spells of Madame Mole to keep it safe. These were uncertain times.

He sat and waited a little more. A few more minutes and he must return the Moonpiece to its rightful place. He had made his decision.

The velvet bag around his neck began to sway again, and as it did so, he saw a green blot appear on the horizon. Elated, he held it in his gaze right up until the moment it deftly landed beside him. The warmth of the dragon's breath heated the air that had become cold by the proximity of the Thworgs.

Together, they carefully calculated the time and energy needed. The blast of moonbeam would last less than a second: there would be only one chance to pierce the veil of black and find the small Shepony. Error would mean certain death for their friend. They, too, would be in grave danger. Either way, the wrath of the Thworgs would be forever sealed against the magic gardens. Thworgs would never forgive anyone who dared steal their prey or intervene in their business. But right was right, and the badness must be challenged.

It was time to leave. Balanced between the shoulders of his mighty friend, they flew towards Rowan Hill. It didn't take long to spot the black swarming cloud that hovered on its eastern side. As the two got closer, still the icy chill made them gasp.

This was the moment - and Monty undid the clasp of the small wooden box that held his Moonpiece. Ian produced an identical box from under his left wing.

Together, they undid the clasps and held what looked like two smoothly flattened oval greyish stones. Ordinary in their appearance, at first they changed rapidly: as if the exposure to each other, even not as yet touching, had lit an enormous and powerful fire. As the two were brought together, an explosion of silver light burst outwards, blasting from within. Monty clung fast to his friend's shoulders, and even the dragon, as big as he was, buckled as it consumed them both.

Together, Monty and Ian concentrated their thoughts, willing the energy into a beam that they could mount. And as they did so, it began to spin and form as they held fast to this vision. The beam formed before them, stretching ahead by several feet. They were ready.

Both were entirely dependent on each other to keep their thoughts focused on the beam's path through the blackness. This was the only speck of goodness in the Thworgs' dark, dark world.

As soon as the spiralling black cloud of Thworgs came into view, the energy of the joined-up Moonpieces was released, and the moonbeam poured forward its silver beam. It cut through the blackness, its sheer force blasting a way in and down.

Poppelana felt something grasp and lift her. She thought that she had succumbed to the awful blackness of the Thworgs. But as we already know, this was not the case. Risking everything, a brave cat and his fine friend the Dragon had carried out a daring rescue!

Chapter Fifteen

The Magic Returns

The party could not truly begin until their leader returned! They did not have long to wait.

Suddenly, a gust of wind blew hot around them and everyone's attention was now held by what they saw in the night sky. Some of the smaller animals pointed and called out: the very size of the dragon always made them gasp.

Here in the night sky, Ian the Chinese dragon seemed even more magnificent as his silhouette crossed the path of the syrup gold moon. How brightly it shone on this special night! Excitement led to squeals of delight as, once again, the familiar green mist of the Chinese dragon puffed around them.

Landing with a gush, his enormous square head faced the crowd and his two travelling companions now became visible to them all.

Released from the safety of the dragon's claw, the little horse shook her body and stood. Beside her was Monty. Just as they had met the first time in the wood, she now pawed the ground three times with her right hoof and bucked her back legs, giving the traditional greeting of a Shepony to a dear friend.

Monty bowed towards her, a look of great pride and joy sweeping across his face. Behind him crowded the animals and creatures of the garden; to the left stood an entire herd of miniature horses who had found a new home. He could not have been happier.

The last of the puddings and pies that were too good to resist were quickly laid out on the wooden logs. Jugs of apple cider and cherry squash were poured into the beech shells by swooping bats. The music from Mr Badger's orchestra began to play more loudly, as the biggest party that the garden had ever had began!

Holly laughed as she watched the tiny stick people dance arm-in-arm with the friendly Greenlings. They formed little circles of eight and span around the garden!

Tom ate at least three of the delicious apple cakes. And Victoria managed to dance with several of the little horses!

Much later, when most of the animals and creatures had gone to bed, the children sat on a wall of green tail provided by a sleepy dragon, with Monty and Poppelana. They chatted excitedly as each recounted their own part in what had taken place. Sooty slept at their feet. In the morning, he would be found snoozing on the front porch by their parents and returned home. Their parents and their neighbours would be overjoyed to have him back after his mysterious disappearance, and would never know how great a part he had played in the big adventure. What had begun with a cycle ride and a great deal of goodwill had ended with an amazing rescue, and lots of new friends.

Holly, realising that they too must go to bed, hugged both of these two brave animals.

'Will everything be all right now, Monty?' she asked.

'The Thworgs cruelly invaded a land that was not theirs,' he said, facing his little friend. 'For this they cannot be forgiven, Holly, and we must be watchful. But here in the magic garden, we are always quite safe!'

Hopping down from the dragon's tail, they now stood right next to his smoky nostrils and golden eyes. Fondly, they patted Ian's large green head, and wished him a safe journey back to the banks of the Yangtze.

'Please come back soon!' Victoria pleaded.

The dragon's crackly voice gave an answer that left the children speechless and intrigued.

'Surely you must visit me next,' he said in a now soft husky voice.

The children now headed into the house and back

to bed, thrilled and hardly able to believe that they had been invited to the only other magic garden in the world! Most of all, they knew how lucky they were to have such wonderful friends.

Monty looked at the moon and pondered the future. The magic in the garden would remain as long as the Moonpiece was safe. Would the Thworgs dare to seek it so that they could harness its energy for evil? Especially now that they knew its inhabitants had helped the Sheponies... He shuddered.

Seeing the intense concentration on Monty's face, Poppelana sought to reassure her friend.

'Nothing stays the same forever,' she whispered.

Monty smiled, and walked with her to the small field at the back of the garden, where her herd were almost all fast asleep. He knew that what she said was true.

After his return, Monty and the Chinese dragon talked together long into the night. They discussed the ancient past, the enemy, and the future because they had both lived a long time and were very wise. Each knew that they may not have seen the last of the evil Thworgs, who they now knew had grown in strength and daring. For now, however, they agreed all was well. There would be many more adventures in both magic gardens!

Ian's body began to shimmer and Monty knew that he was preparing to leave.

'Thanks alone are not enough,' Monty said, as he lent close to his friend. 'Our lives are embroidered together with the strongest thread of friendship, loyalty and respect.'

In response, a warm, glowing look covered the dragon's fine features.

Before his final farewell, Ian the magic dragon made Monty promise one thing: that he too would come to his home where the other small piece of the moon had landed thousands of years ago.

'Come and experience some of its wonders!' he crackled enthusiastically.

Then, with a blue flash that illuminated the garden like a sheet of lightening, he was gone on his solitary flight home. Dragons always enjoy a little bit of time on their own.

Unbeknown to Monty, it would not be that long before he and three small children undertook a very long journey to China. And more specifically, to the banks of the Yangtze and the other magic garden that nestled there!

But that is definitely a story for another day.